# The Cursed Jewel

Other works by this author:

*Final Flight of the Ranegr*
*The Starlight Lancer*
*The Awakening*
*Path of a Hero*
*Metanoia*
*The Star Warriors*

Find them online at
**https://www.cscooper.com.au/books**

# The Cursed Jewel

C. S. Cooper

For my speech and drama teachers. I wouldn't have my writing skills without your tutelage.

# CONTENTS

# Acknowledgements

I acknowledge Atsushi Oukubo, whose manga inspired this story. I also thank the people who read my novel, *Final Flight of the Ranegr*. Since you were so intrigued by *The AXOM Saga,* and requested paperback copies, here you go. Then, there are my parents and family, who encouraged me to publish it.

# 1 | Moonlit Hunt

A crescent Moon ruled the night, yet the Las Vegas air simmered with heat leftover from the daytime. Bright lights illuminated the sleepless burlesque city, affording few shadows in which one could hide. And yet, the most sinister critters can always find a hiding place for their latest victim.

Police tape cordoned off a dark alley riddled with the flashes of cameras. Those cameras diligently recorded every marker, every measurement, every tiny detail of the gutted corpse. Its blood slowly trickled along the concrete, and the CSI just knew clean up would be a pain. He lowered his camera as the police captain approached, yawning not only at the lateness of the hour.

"What've we got here?" asked the captain, his face casting a bored expression the way of the dead body.

"Latino female, age approximately thirty-five, multiple deep lacerations up through the midsection," said the CSI, bemused at how anyone could not be disturbed by the grizzly sight. He pointed to the spatter across the walls, and the long red trail that stretched down the alleyway. "My guess, it was a single hit with tremendous force. She was caught by surprise, and was thrown through the air. Most likely dead before she hit the ground."

The captain's eyebrows twitched. "What kind of perp do you think this is, son?"

The CSI did his best to hide his thoughts, certain the captain would think him insane. He resisted the urge to touch the thin-chain bangle around his wrist. He just shrugged, "It's only my preliminary analysis, sir. I'll have a full report once I've analysed the photos."

"Do we know who the victim is at least?" asked the captain.

A female CSI stood up from the corpse and sheathed a swab. "We'll run DNA back at the lab."

The captain sighed, "Well then, don't let me keep you." And he promptly left to deal with the first wave of reporters come for a scoop.

The CSI remained motionless, his eyes gazed upwards in subtle amusement. His colleague approached him and murmured, "This'll be another cold case, I'm sure."

"But *they'll* get the bastard that did this," said the CSI.

His colleague eyed the bangle around her wrist, and smirked. "Who do you think *they'll* be? The rock-star ninja?"

"Nah!" exclaimed the CSI with a chuckle. He glanced at her, a twinkle in his eye. "It'll be the blonde."

\* \* \*

If the Moon had eyes, it would have wept blood. Its pale light reflected off the wight's finger-blades. It edged out of the shadows, and drooled hungrily at the sight of its next meal: a woman heading home, having finished her day of work in questionable professions. Only one aspect of her attracted the creature: not the way she gripped the pepper spray can in her purse, surrounded by hundreds of dollars in tips; not her tight jeans and shirt bringing out her shapely curves; not her pretty face covered in flaking makeup; not the ballsy, no-nonsense attitude her expression radiated by default.

It was her soul, and it looked delicious.

The beast leapt out of the shadows and descended the fire escape, its razor-sharp blades at the ready. The woman heard its approach, swivelled, and unleashed her mace. Crumpled cash went everywhere as she sprayed the creature, but the caustic fluid only struck its metal mask. The creature leapt at her, its heels impacting her chest and sending her to the ground. It towered over her, relished the horror radiating from her soul, and raised its claws for the kill.

A slurping sound pierced the air, carrying with it the signature of an oh-so-much sweeter target. The creature's lidless eyes flashed purple behind its mask as it eyed the duo standing under a streetlight nearby.

Terrified, the woman fled, leaving behind much of her nightly haul, but the creature couldn't have cared less. It crouched, its pale skin quivering at the sensation of the two most tasty-looking souls it had ever seen.

The albino stepped forward and cracked his knuckles.

"So, Maka," he chuckled as he wiped away his own drool. He grinned, bearing his sharp incisors at the creature. "You ready to get back in the game?"

"I was born ready, Soul," intoned the blonde pigtailed girl, her green eyes flashing brighter than the creature before them.

At that, Soul's body dematerialised into a pair of energetic beams that encircled Maka. Their paths entwined into a helix, which solidified into the handle of a monstrous red and black scythe. Maka glared at the creature and snarled, "Servant Girl Annihilator[1], your soul is mine!"

The creature hissed and scampered forward like a spider. It brought its claws for a brutal uppercut. Maka twirled her scythe and blocked the blows with lightning speed. She could smell the alarm that filled the creature, and grinned with glee. She gave a holler as she spun on the spot, swiping across the creature's midsection. The lithe beast managed to backflip over her blow, and backed away

---

[1]  An unidentified serial killer who terrorized Austin, Texas, between 1884 and 1885.

to gain some ground.

Maka pressed her attack. She lunged forward, and swiped upward from the creature's right. It darted aside and brought a slash to Maka's right, which she blocked with the handle of her scythe. The creature targeted her exposed back, but she reached over her shoulders with the scythe and parried the blow. She hooked the scythe blade onto the monster's armoured wrist and wrenched it over her head. She then locked the blade under the dazed monster's legs, and flipped it onto its back.

The wight shrieked with panic as Maka swung the scythe over her head. With a triumphant roar, she brought the tip of the blade down through the monster's black mouth. The thing gurgled with pain, and its body started to contort and quiver. Its pale thick hide split at the seams and disintegrated in a flash of purple light that coalesced into a sphere of burning matter.

The scythe slid out of Maka's hands, grew arms and legs, and morphed back into the form of her albino friend. Soul grabbed the squishy lump, licking his lips ravenously as he slurped the thing down his gullet.

He sighed with contentment, while Maka gagged.

"Seriously, is it *that* important that you physically eat the souls?" she asked.

"I'm Soul Eater!" exclaimed Soul. "It's my trademark. Plus …" He picked his teeth with his pinkie nail. "They got a nice texture to them."

"Ugh," moaned Maka. "I can't believe we have to do this ninety-eight more times."

"Ninety-nine," reminded Soul. "Don't forget the Witch's soul too."

At that, Maka cringed at the memory of a cat's soul sliding down Soul's throat. Her body tightened up with fury and frustration, and she started kicking a nearby trashcan.

"God-Ducking-Fammit!" she exclaimed. "How could I have missed that? She looked like a Witch, but I should have known Blaire was just a cat. I should have been able to sense it!"

It had been disappointing for both of them. They had their ninety-nine dark souls, known as Asura Eggs. It had taken months of hunting the names on the Reaper's list of evil-doers, and they finally obtained the ninety-nine souls. Then all that remained was a Witch's soul, and Soul would have reached his full power. Maka would have become a wielder of a Death Scythe, the highest honour among their ranks!

They found an alleged Witch, named Blaire, and reaped her soul. But just as Soul swallowed that spirit, they found Blaire had in fact *not* been a Witch, but a magical cat. They took one of her nine lives, and collected a cat soul instead! Not only did that ruin Soul's appetite, and have him choking on ethereal hairballs, but it lost them all their ninety-nine souls. They had to start all over again thanks to that mistake.

Both of them had been demoralised for weeks.

His own disappointment notwithstanding, Soul had to admit he loved watching Maka's tantrums. He made a mental note to hide her copy of *Cloud Atlas*, just to see her reaction. Then he walked over to her, put his hands on her shoulders, and began his Maka Calming Ritual.

"It's okay, Maka," he cooed. "*Goosfraba … Goosfraba …*"

Maka pursed her lips, fury crackling up her spine at the sound of Soul's attempts at a soothing voice. It was like nails on a chalkboard, and she swatted him away.

"It's alright, I'm okay now," she grumbled.

Soul shot her back a sharp-toothed grin, which only got on her nerves even more. She grasped for a lifeline in her mind, and remembered why they were in that alleyway to begin with.

With a deep breath, she smiled and said, "So, we managed to get a soul without much problem. We should report back."

Soul checked his watch. "Oh yeah, I've got those tests to grade before tomorrow too."

Maka groaned, "Agh, and I've got to get my lesson plans for next semester done too!"

Soul caught Maka before she could go on another rant about their busy schedule. He didn't keep her from grumbling as they left the alleyway and walked across the road, toward an empty storefront. Maka was still fuming as they stood in front of the glass windows, and didn't realise where they were until Soul blurted, "Do you want me to open the doorway?"

Maka looked around, and sheepishly stammered, "No, I'll do it." She breathed on the glass and cast a fog over it. Then she wrote a sequence of numbers into it.

"Four-two-four-two-five-six-four," she recited.

As the numbers on the glass flickered with ethereal light, a question bubbled up though Soul's mind. It was one that had bothered him for a long while.

"Why did the Reaper pick this access number?" he wondered aloud.

Maka shrugged, "I hear this number freaks out Japanese[2] people."

"What? So it's to get back at the Japanese?" exclaimed Soul.

"Well, it *was* Japanese Alchemists that invented the Kakugane," replied Maka. "Look where that got us."

"Yeah, Maka, not everyone's as down with history as you are," snapped Soul.

Before Maka could go on her history tirade, the entire panel of glass started to glow. A high-pitched ding sounded, and the glowing glass faded to reveal a portal into a brightly lit room. The pair stepped through it as naturally as if they had stepped into their shared apartment. The portal sealed behind them, and they sighed at the feeling of cool air on their skin.

---

[2]    When read in Japanese, the number sequence reads *shi-ni-shi-ni-go-ro-shi*, which sounds like "Die, Die, Kill."

Their portal disappeared, leaving behind a mirror. It distorted their reflections, making their heads miniscule compared to the cartoon-esque skull emblazoned on the red stone-paved floor.

One of the other mirrors in the circular room lit up. In stepped a black-haired Asian girl almost too tall to fit through the portal. She brushed lint and dirt off her pale yellow dress, and her eyes lit up excitedly when she saw Maka and Soul. With a gleam in her eye, she proclaimed, "Introducing the greatest great man of all time, known for his unholy greatness. The God of the future, Black-Star!"

Through the portal swooped a boy in baggy white pants and a sleeveless black shirt that showed off his well-built physique. He howled with excitement as he hit the ground with, what he thought to be, enough force to crack the planet in half.

"Black-Star is in the mutha-truckin' building!" he roared.

His loud holler echoed down the hallway, leaving only silence. The only applauding crowd was the one in his head.

"Star, what up, man?" exclaimed Soul as he bumped fists with the shorter boy.

"Soul! We dun did it!" bellowed Black-Star, slinging his arms around the much taller Asian girl's midsection. "Ain't that right, Tsubaki?"

Tsubaki's shoulders reached for her ears as she beamed excitedly. "We finally got a soul!"

"Really?" cried Maka with delight. She threw her arms around Tsubaki. "Congratulations!"

"Maka and I just got a soul too," said Soul. He patted Black-Star on the shoulder and hollered, "It'll be a race between us to see who gets to the Death Scythe level first."

Black-Star scoffed and cast Soul's hand away. "I could never race someone for anything. If I did, my assured victory would just crush you. I couldn't do that to my bestest besties, could I?"

Maka grimaced and murmured, "I'm sure we could handle it."

Black-Star clapped his hands together. "Well then, it's, like, eleven at night. What say we get our grub on? Y'all need to hear the exploits of Black-Star and Tsubaki, right?"

"Word to that," replied Soul. The boys sauntered off down the hall, the girls in tow. Tsubaki wore an excited grin, dampened only by the dirt and scuffs on her face. Maka cringed at the late night that was certain to follow.

\* \* \*

In a white room, a mirror stood on a dais surrounded by black grave markers. In front of that mirror stood a figure, cloaked in black mist that obscured his every feature save for the childish skull mask that was his face. He studied the mirror, which showed a moving image of the four people who had just arrived through the portals.

"Two successful missions," intoned the figure with a squeaky voice. Then he swivelled and clapped his big, white-gloved hands together. "I think I've got your team mates, Kiddo!"

In the chair sat a black-suited teen, his hands threaded together on his lap. His face was expressionless as he glared at the image. Then he croaked, "There are indeed two of each gender, and indeed two of meister and weapon."

His body's trembling reached a zenith and he shot to his feet. He outstretched a finger at the mirror and screamed, "But that Japanese girl is too freaking tall!"

## 2 | Asymmetry

Every photon the sun threw felt like a boulder. They relentlessly struck the heads of the three figures that stood atop the building. The horizon rippled with mirages, thanks only to the sheer heat of the desert.

The tall blonde fanned herself with her cowgirl hat, and loosened the collar of her red sleeveless turtleneck. She was grateful it exposed her belly, giving her some respite from the heat. She was equally grateful that she and her companions were standing on a roof, out of reach of prying eyes.

Beside her, a shorter blonde girl swooned at the sight of the Giza Necropolis. "Ain't it a sight? Them's look like big piles!"

"Patty!" growled the slender, black-clad teen between them. "They aren't piles. They are pyramids." He blushed. "And what a testament to symmetry they are."

"Testify!" exclaimed Patty as she punched the air above her head. Her blurt made the taller girl nervous.

"Patty, quiet down!" she chided as she tried to stifle the hyperactive girl.

"What's the matter, Liz?" asked Patty.

"Weren't you listening on the way over?" murmured Liz. "Here in Egypt, us girls'd get shot for dressin' this way." She looked over at their third friend. "Hey, Kiddo, why aren't we, ya know, dressed more appropriately?"

The boy, whose full name was Death The Kid, narrowed his yellow eyes at them.

"Because you insisted on belly shirts, Liz," he snapped. He looked them both up and down. Something snapped in his head and he growled, "And yet, despite my best efforts, you still are not symmetrical!" He thrust his finger in Liz's face. "You're too tall and your breasts are too small!" He loomed over Patty. "And *you're* too short, and your breasts are too big!"

He proceeded to pace frantically, tearing at his hair.

"It'd be better if Liz's breasts were bigger than Patty's, but this is maddening!" Then he suddenly stopped, his eyes unfocused, and a tiny epiphany struck him. He clapped his hands together and cried, "That's right! Breast augmentation for the elder, growth hormone for the younger. Yes! Then my weapon partners would truly be identical, therefore symmetrical!"

Liz narrowed her eyes and snarled, "Snowball's chance in Hell, Kiddo."

Kiddo suddenly hunched over, and his body shook. He growled, "It's the only way for you two to be truly symmetrical, just like those Pyramids! Perfection supreme! You must do it, for my sake!"

Patty scratched her head and mumbled, "I don't wanna do gross homophone."

Kiddo's knees lost all energy, and he collapsed in a twitching fit of mania. Tears burst from his eyes as he bashed the concrete roof hard enough to crack it.

"My life is meaningless! I'm trash! I'm scum! I'm dirty!" he wailed. "There is nothing if I cannot have symmetry!"

Patty fell on the floor laughing. Meanwhile, Liz rubbed the bridge of her nose irately and sighed. She crouched down and patted the teen's head. She gently said, "It's alright, Kiddo. You're alright. You're not scum, or trash, or dirty."

"And your life means lots," bellowed Patty jovially as she bounced up and down on her knees.

Kiddo sniffed back his tears and looked up into the girls' faces.

"You really think so?" he stammered.

"Of course," said Liz. "Plus, we're plenty symmetrical in our weapon forms, right?"

"Right!" exclaimed Patty.

Kiddo shot to his feet and waltzed to the edge of the roof, his face completely dry.

"Well then, transform and we'll get to work," he curtly ordered.

*Goddamn bi-polar nut-job rich kid,* thought Liz as she and Patty dematerialised in a flash. Their light morphed into twin pistols in Kiddo's hands. He gripped them tightly as his eyes scanned the entire Giza Necropolis. Those yellow orbs narrowed keenly as they zoned in on a patch of land to the south of the Pyramids.

"Liz, Patty, I'll need a hand here," he mumbled. His eyes closed, and he reached out with his mind, connecting with their souls. The nerves along his arms crackled with their shared energy, which he focused outward. His senses attuned, he reached outward with ethereal antennae, unknown to humans yet unique to *his* species. His mental olfactory senses tingled with the sensation of their target, and he leapt from the roof.

A hover-board appeared out of thin air beneath Kiddo's feet. It carried him into the desert. He accelerated over the searing sands, the sensation drawing him like a bee to nectar. He couldn't care less that his quarry saw him on approach. A rabble of grave robbers of their ilk was hardly a match for him.

One of the sentries caught sight of him and bellowed, "Meister!" He cocked his machine gun and fired. The few shots lucky enough to find their mark, Kiddo easily deflected with the impregnable barrels of his guns. He spun in mid-air, targeted the gunman, and unleashed two shots of pure energy that sent the man headfirst into an ancient pillar. Kiddo came in hot, skidding to a halt in the middle of the monument.

As he twirled his guns about his fingers, he proclaimed, "Ladies! Shall we dance?"

The girls' voices burst from the guns.

"Let's," quipped Liz.

"Boogie!" exclaimed Patty.

Kiddo took out the panicked robber to his left, before darting out of the path of another who came at his right. As he twirled in the air, he brought his foot across his attacker's face while unleashing shot after shot at the men fleeing the site. The energy bullets struck the hapless burglars and sent them writhing to the ground.

The otherworldly scent of a weapon transformation tickled at Kiddo's nose, and he turned to see a cloaked man charging him. The attacker's forearm morphed into a chainsaw, which he swiped at Kiddo's head. Kiddo dodged the blow, tossed Liz into the air and with his now-free hand socked the man in the face. He caught Liz, thrust her barrel under the dazed man's chin, and fired. The blast sent the man through the air and he struck the ground hard.

Kiddo looked around, his guns at the ready for any more attackers. But he, Liz, and Patty could sense something was off.

"Hey, Kiddo," said Patty. "Wasn't these guys s'posed to be neckie-mancers?"

"Necromancers, Patty," said Liz. "But you're right. Our blows aren't exposing their souls."

"Which means they're not Asura Eggs," said Kiddo, his frown deepening. He eyed the man with the chainsaw hand, and mumbled, "I wonder how many of them are Demon Weapons as well." He waltzed toward the unconscious man and studied him a moment. He edged Patty's barrel toward the man's hood and pushed it aside. A faint white patch peaked out from under the man's collar, radiating outwards like a venomous insect bite. Kiddo pulled the collar down further to reveal the centre of the blemish, which pulsated with a deep green hue.

"Looks like he's rotten there," said Patty.

"Hey, if he's a Demon Weapon, wouldn't he be registered with DWMA?" mumbled Liz. His curiosity piqued further, Kiddo checked the man's wrists and found a bracelet with the Reaper's skull logo engraved into its outer surface. On the underside, it read, 'Mario Ferrone, N.O.T. Class of 1985.'

"What the Hell?" exclaimed Liz.

"I thought N.O.T. students didn't do fightin'," intoned Patty.

Kiddo stood and glanced at the entrance to the tomb the men were robbing. He edged toward the opening in the bedrock, the smell of millennia-stale air wafting upward from within. He edged down the eroding staircase and moved along the dark corridor. His yellow eyes glimmered enough to light his way, but it wasn't enough to stop the gun in his left hand from shuddering.

"God, Kiddo, do we have to go through the dark?" mumbled Liz. "You know how I feel about dark places, and mummies too."

"Ha ha ha! Big-Sis is a big sissie!" giggled Patty, her weapon form bouncing around in Kiddo's right hand.

Liz protested, "I am not! I just –"

"What? Ya think Imhotep is gonna eat your eyes?" chortled Patty.

"Patty! Don't remind me of that movie!" shrieked Liz.

"Quiet! Both of you!" snapped Kiddo. They reached the end of the tunnel, which led into a large chamber. Kiddo sniffed the light rods laid about the cavern and judged that they'd just been switched off. His keen eyes scanned the room. "I know someone's here. Show yourself and I'll be merciful."

A soft voice reverberated through the stone chamber. It rose above the faint tickle of trickling sand grains. It drew Kiddo's attention to the man emerging from behind one of the sarcophagi. The hooded figure held his splayed hand before him, and a glimmering vortex of energetic streaks formed in his palm. His voice grew louder, even as Kiddo pointed his guns and fired repeated blasts that dinged harmlessly off a magical shield.

"That's our necktie monger?" mumbled Patty.

"That's him," spat Liz.

The man clenched his fist around the energy swirl and hurled it into the floor. The room lit up as the energy flooded the area surrounding the sarcophagi. Tendrils of glimmering red light clambered up the sides of the stone caskets and slithered through their seams. Moments later, the heavy stone lids, unmoved for centuries, burst into the air and shattered.

Liz trembled, "Oh no, Kiddo, we're not gonna have."

"Mummies!" exclaimed Patty with a much too excited tone.

Kiddo looked out from under his raised forearms and wafted away the dust that rained down on him. A dozen tightly wrapped bodies sat erect in the sarcophagi, red-glowing dots where their eyes should have been. They made no sound as they rose to their feet. They tore away their bandages to reveal their thousand-years-dry flesh, stretched out their decrepit limbs, and then fixed their demonic eyes on the gunman before them.

The undead charged Kiddo, screeching gutturally. He scoffed with disgust and twirled his guns around his fingers.

"Let's go, girls!" he barked.

"Roger!" exclaimed Patty.

Liz whimpered, "Let's get this done quick."

Kiddo dropped to the floor, kicked the feet out from under one of the mummies, and unleashed a barrage into its stomach. As his first victim dematerialised into a floating soul, Kiddo was already in motion on the next one, pistol-whipping the ghoul so hard its head flew off. The next one, he got in the groin, before somersaulting over it and firing a bolt down the length of its spine. He landed in front of the next, and shoved his left-hand gun into its mouth.

"Gah! Don't put me in its mouth, damn it!" cried Liz as her barrel unleashed an ethereal bullet through the monster's head.

As the mummies charged, the necromancer withdrew to the back of the burial chamber. He unfortunately hadn't noticed the remaining magical tendrils flowing into the opulent, gold-plated sarcophagus that lay on the dais. Its lid did not erupt like the others, but rather creaked open, ever so gently, as its occupant sensed his presence. A white, gnarled hand slithered out, grabbed him by the head, and dragged him inside before he could scream. The sounds of munching and slurping were barely audible over the gunfire and crashes of Kiddo's battle.

The mummies vanquished, Kiddo stood amid a ruined burial chamber surrounded by the blood-red souls of his victims. He held out his guns and said, "Six each, girls. We must have symmetry."

"Got it," droned Liz.

As the souls gravitated toward the gun barrels, Patty intoned, "Hey, Kiddo, what about that neck-mingie?"

Kiddo swivelled in search of the necromancer, but saw nobody else. He heard no one else's breathing, save for his own and those of his weapons. His eyes caught a small glimmer of something beside the sarcophagus on the dais. Studying it, he saw it was another N.O.T. bracelet.

"Ted Caldicot, N.O.T. Class of 1990," he read aloud. His pale brow furrowed. "Are all these guys former N.O.T. students? What the Hell is going on?"

"Kiddo! Watch out!" cried Liz.

Beside him, the sarcophagus pitched upward until it stood on its feet. Kiddo leapt into the air and dodged a flurry of razor-sharp ribbons. The ribbons flicked and lashed at him, uncaring if they damaged anything or brought down the roof. Kiddo finally found an opening in the onslaught to point his guns at the coffin.

He froze.

"Kiddo! What's the matter?" exclaimed Liz.

Kiddo stammered breathlessly, "I can't!" Tears trickled from his enamoured eyes as he beheld the ornate, gold-plated sarcophagus. He gasped, "It's so symmetrical!"

"Uh-oh," droned Patty.

The ribbons came at him, full-blast.

"Watch out!" cried Liz.

Blood erupted from Kiddo's mouth as the ribbons slashed through his abdomen. The eyes of the sarcophagus, perfect in Kiddo's neurotic view, glimmered red as a deep voice bellowed, "Feel my wrath! Wrath of the Pharaoh!"

Kiddo's guns flashed and took the form of Liz and Patty. Frantically, they hooked their arms under his and scrambled back down the passage. The sarcophagus issued another barrage of sharp tentacles, which lunged after the trio. Ancient limestone bricks crumpled under the force, and the ceiling above their heads shuddered. Behind them, the tunnel started to collapse. A gust of air blasted them the rest of the way, and they landed face-first in the hot Egyptian sand.

Kiddo stained the sand with his blood as Liz and Patty struggled to shoulder him. The sarcophagus rose out of the rubble and hung in the air. Kiddo swooned, "Ah! Pharaoh of Symmetry! It is an honour to be disembowelled by you!"

"No, it's not!" screamed Liz as she pulled at his arms.

The sarcophagus' seams cracked, and the creature within grumbled, "I shall take care of this, with my true power!" The lid swung open, and the entity within emerged. Its elongated body flagellated the air around its eye-less head, which bore a mound of folded skin that hung open like a great maw. From its left side sprouted two long, muscular arms with spindly digits capable of crushing diamond. From its right sprouted a dozen of its ribbon tentacles.

Time stood still. Kiddo's yellow eyes narrowed. He closed one eye, and studied one side. He closed the other eye, and studied the other. He kept doing that, over and over, while Liz and Patty exchanged excited glances.

"Here it comes," mumbled Patty with a giggle.

With a rage-fuelled flash of energy, Kiddo's wounds sealed. The white lines girdling half his head shimmered as he roared, "You asymmetric slime bucket! You're all messed up!"

He held out his hands, and Liz and Patty took their rightful place there as his loyal weapons. He leapt above the beast's lunging hands, and unleashed a hundred energetic gunshots into it. The entity's limbs disintegrated. It countered with the ribbons, but Kiddo was far too quick. He darted aside, and dislocated the entire set of ribbons where they met the thing's body. Standing on its shoulders, he pushed the barrels of his guns into the bewildered creature's slick hide, and fired shot after shot after shot into its head.

Kiddo stood over the ruined site, its ancient secrets lost for all time. He sneered as the beast's wretched form evaporated in the desert winds, and spat in disgust. The men they'd fought before had disappeared, no doubt having run off.

Liz and Patty returned to human form, and followed Kiddo out into the desert. The girls watched their meister as he trudged along, lost in thought.

"Hey, Kiddo," cooed Liz. "You still upset about that asymmetric thingie? Never mind. You got it now."

"And we've gotta buncha souls too!" exclaimed Patty.

"That's not what bothers me," mumbled Kiddo. He turned and faced them. "The people raiding this tomb were N.O.T. graduates. And if I remember right, they'd gone missing a few months ago. They show up here, with necromancer abilities, trying to raid a tomb containing a larval Old One."

Liz and Patty exchanged glances. The younger

shrugged, clearly not following anything their meister had said.

"So, you think something's happening?" asked Liz.

Kiddo pursed his lips as he thought some more.

"Those men had a strange mark, like they'd been stung," said Kiddo. "I'm thinking mind control. Someone's brainwashing N.O.T. graduates into an army."

"That's bad," exclaimed Liz. "There's way more N.O.T.s than E.A.T.s. We'll have to find them and stop them."

Kiddo grinned. "Of course. But we can't do it alone."

# 3 | Morning Mayhem

The morning sun hung just above the horizon and blasted light across the barren scape of Death Valley, Nevada. But the people within the confines of Death City had no concern for the blistering heat. The city's weather was a comfy seventy-four degrees, thanks to the Reaper's secure barrier, which scintillated the light that crept gently into Maka's bedroom.

The girl had been up since seven, already done with her morning yoga, shower, and breakfast. Her lesson plans for the term sat ready on her desk, and her daily planner read, 'Demonstration for N.O.T. Orientation. Make sure Soul is ready!'

Maka had plenty of time to get her lazy weapon partner ready, and so was more than content to take her time with the package in front of her. It had arrived just in time for orientation, and her heart fluttered with excitement as she slid it open. Inside was her pair of brand-new, black Converse shoes. She delicately took one out and studied it with a joyous face. She inhaled the new shoe smell, and her eyes glazed over with merriment.

*Now, time for the first wear!*

She slipped on some socks and slid her feet into the shoes. They were a tight fit at first. Once her feet were in and they were laced up, she stood and smiled contently at the extra inch they added to her height. She threw on her black overcoat and gazed into her full-length mirror.

Her checkerboard skirt, cream-coloured cardigan, her black overcoat, her blonde pigtails, and her brand new Converse shoes.

*I rock!*

Maka heard a shriek and a crash. Her bedroom door flew open and in charged Soul. Blood dribbled from his nose. Soapy shower water dripped off his body, over which he held a towel with one hand. In the other, he held a black cat, which he shoved in her face.

"Maka! What the Hell is Blaire still doing here!?" he bellowed.

Flabbergasted, Maka could find no words to say to the cat that giggled flirtatiously.

"I wanted to have a shower with Soul," the cat chirped.

Soul threw the cat onto the bed and yelled, "So you hide in the bathroom and try to jump me?"

The cat chirped an incantation, and in a flash morphed into a voluptuous black-haired beauty. She made a show of faux shame as she provocatively shimmied her hips, which made Soul nearly pass out.

She moaned, "Soul's rugged body made me so hot! I just *had* to have him!"

The image of Soul in the shower made Maka blush. She looked to the cat-turned-human and snarled, "Blaire, what was the condition of you staying with us?"

Blaire pouted, "Fully clothed at all times, and no trying to molest Soul."

"Get out of here and put some clothes on, damn it!" snapped Maka. Blaire eyed the blonde girl with a lewd glimmer. Before she could open her mouth, Maka yelled, "Not a chance!"

Blaire sighed with disappointment and left the room. Soul turned to Maka.

"I still don't know why she's here," he said. "It's *her* fault that we lost all our ninety-nine souls."

Maka just stared at Soul. He raved a little longer, and

stopped when Maka waltzed to her bookshelf and procured a heavy illustrated copy of *The Silmarillion*. With frantic savagery, she swatted him over the head with it, bellowing, "Get out of my room and get dressed!"

Soul fled from the room, almost losing his towel in the process. He made a beeline for the bathroom. Blaire stood beside the door in a towel, blowing him kisses.

"*I'll* never hit you like that," she cooed.

"Screw you, Blaire!" bellowed Soul as he slammed the bathroom door shut.

Blaire moaned, "But that's what I want!"

Maka shut the door to her bedroom. She saw Soul's watery footprints, water droplets on her teaching materials, cat moult on her bed, and soapy splatter all over her brand new Converse shoes. She rubbed her temples to banish her stress, knowing her demonstration to the N.O.T. students would not be easy.

*He must pay for this!*

Soul took his time in the shower, during which Blaire kept vigil in her cat form beside the bathroom door. When he emerged, he made no effort to avoid stepping on Blaire's tail. He gingerly towelled his hair dry, wincing as his hand passed over the lumps on his head where Maka had clobbered him. His attacker sat on the couch munching at a bowl of corn flakes and chuckling at last night's episode of *John Oliver*. He shot her the evils as he strutted to the kitchen and scanned the fridge for the milk.

Only a few drops remained.

"Maka! Why didn't you get milk last night?" he wailed.

"Didn't need any," snorted the blonde. When he brandished the near-empty carton, she vindictively chuckled, "I was hungry and so had seconds on breakfast."

Soul growled furiously at her demure smile, concealing the cruel prankster within. He threw on his jacket and headed for the door. Over his shoulder, he snapped, "Anything else we need from the shop?"

Blaire scratched her twitching ears and chimed, "Could

you get some batteries for me?"

Soul's eyes narrowed and he quipped, "What would a cat need batteries?"

"A girl has her toys," murmured the cat lasciviously. Maka smacked her head.

Soul turned with a sigh and headed toward the door, which suddenly burst from its hinges and came down on his face. Standing on the destroyed hardwood door was Black-Star, his eyes bloodshot from over-exertion.

"Soul!" he bellowed. "I found that a-hole what stole our glory!" He glanced around the apartment, finding only a bored Blaire and a flummoxed Maka. He proceeded to jump up and down, yelling, "Soul! Your God of all supreme Godliness calls upon thee! Where is Soul!? I must have my Soul!?"

Maka finally cried, "You're standing on him, you jackass!"

Black-Star gazed down. Soul's twitching hand reached feebly out from under the door. He grunted with dismay as Black-Star leapt off the door, the recoil pushing his ribs to near breaking point. The hyperactive boy threw the door aside as if it were made of cardboard and screamed, "Soul! I found him!"

Soul's body was one big bruise, his nose oozed blood, and he was certain that he had a concussion. He managed to look up at Black-Star's bloodshot, manic gaze, and droned, "Who?"

"Remember, two weeks back, that mutha-trucka who sniped them grave robbin' necromancers?" yelled Black-Star.

"Yeah, we coulda got a hundred souls apiece from that job," said Soul.

"I found him! He's comin' to the school today!" shouted Black-Star.

Soul's concussion cleared in an instant and he shot to his feet. "You're kiddin' me! Let's go get him!"

They vanished down the hall. Maka stood, utterly

bewildered, in the middle of the wrecked apartment. She hadn't even the chance to remind Soul of their demonstration class. As she eyed the cracks in their entrance and the trashed front door, she wondered how she'd fix this in time for school. She shook her head with dismay.

She looked down at her shoes, and edged her foot to avoid a drop of milk from her bowl. She smiled, thankful that she'd at least accomplished something that morning – even if it was just keeping her brand new Converse shoes a tad cleaner.

# 4 | Orientation Day

**M**aka trotted along the main road toward the centre of Death City. She sighed with relief, glad that her building manager had been so quick to call in a repairman for the door. A part of her mind wondered why Black-Star's antics hadn't angered her as much as one would expect.

*Meh, when you grow up with someone, you expect the crazy,* she concluded upon boarding the rail-tram. She gazed out the back of the carriage, down the hill from the foot of which spanned the entirety of the Reaper's city. Tree groves and parks pockmarked the concrete cityscape, the buildings of which were painted in manifold colours. Beyond the walls of the city lay the scorching Nevada desert – a stark contrast to the pleasant metropolis that, rumour had it, the Reaper had modelled after San Francisco.

Maka couldn't help but wonder why.

The tram levelled out at the top of the hill, and ground to a halt. The conductor announced, "Here we are, DWMA. Students alight here."

Maka jumped off the carriage and darted away with all-speed. A stampede of eager kids followed in her wake, and they trembled in awe of the gigantic building before them. Maka could see why they were impressed.

The main entrance was a white sculpture of a skull, yet its cartoonish style – especially the slanting of the eyeholes

– made for quite a welcoming countenance. The skull leaned against the triangular wall that encircled the inner ward, the keep rising above the rest of the castle like an arm reaching for the sky. The towers at each corner of the outer walls looked like gigantic candles, their wicks spewing out holographic flames in vibrant colours. It was like a laser show that, even in the light of day, put the *Freemont Street Experience*[3] to shame.

Maka skipped ahead of the excited rabble of freshmen and made for the entrance. Her ears pricked with the sound of an excited voice exclaiming, "That's Maka Albarn!" She involuntarily swivelled to see a little girl pointing at her. The child bellowed, "She's the Death Scythe's daughter! She's the best scythe-meister of this entire school!" A bunch of kids girdled the child, their mouths agape with amazement.

Maka's brow twitched imperceptibly with the mention of 'Death Scythe.' In the next instant, she chuckled gauchely and gave the newbies the peace sign.

"You all excited for your first day here?" she asked.

Most of the kids nodded excitedly, though a few seemed a bit perturbed by their situation. One of them, a boy in a red shirt emblazoned with the word 'bazinga,' spoke up. "It's a little weird that we're being taught by the Grim Reaper. I mean, ain't he what kills people?"

Maka smiled and crouched down to the kid's level. She said, "Nah! The Reaper isn't mean like that. People used to mistake him for that, and the image just stuck. But he's here to help you." She eyed the boy's nametag, which said 'weapon' under his name. "You've got some amazing powers. And here, at the Demon Weapon Meister Academy, we'll show you how to use those powers for everyone."

The boy cringed, backing away a little and absentmindedly scrunching his shirt. He mumbled, "I

---

[3]    A pedestrian mall in Las Vegas, Nevada, known for its vibrant light
      displays.

don't wanna be a *weapon*."

"You don't have to be," said Maka, gently patting the boy on the head. "We'll show you how to control those powers, so you can be whatever you want to be." She eyed the kids beside the boy and added, "Plus, you're gonna make a tonne of friends while you're here."

As if it were a cue, the girl that had pointed her out before shuffled over and took hold of his tensed hand. The boy shot her a look, and was rewarded with a smile.

"See! You've already made one!" exclaimed Maka. She looked at the other kids in the group. "You're all gonna have fun here, I promise you that!"

She turned away and jogged up the stairs toward the entrance, and the kids let out a fanfare as she left. Their hooting and cheering widened her smile, and she breathed deep of the faint smell of jasmine that flooded the halls of DWMA.

* * *

A conspicuous absence dashed Maka's fleeting good mood. She ticked and fidgeted as the hour hand on her watch veered toward nine. Yet, amid the rabble of students trickling into the classroom, she could not find her partner for the demonstration.

*Where the Hell is Soul!?* She thought.

The last of the students plonked down on the chairs lining the window side of the classroom. Silence overtook the group and grew awkward with every infuriating tick of the clock. Maka wrung her hands nervously as she faced the students.

"Okay, umm," she stammered. "Welcome to the Demon Weapon Meister Academy. I will be your instructor. My name's Maka Albarn. Nice to meet you!"

The gauche children murmured a half-hearted 'hello.'

"I'm sure you understand what a Demon Weapon is, right?" Maka asked. When no one responded, she picked a kid at the front to answer.

"A Demon Weapon is a person who can change into a weapon ... or something?" the student responded.

"Exactly," said Maka. "Do you know what a Demon Weapon does?" It took almost a full minute for the child to shake his head and sit down. Maka forced a smile. "That's alright. A Demon Weapon and a Meister work together to hunt down Asura Eggs. These are the souls of evil-doers. We must stop them before they hatch and cause chaos." A few worried expressions popped up in the class, and sweat started to bead above Maka's hairline. "But, that's only for the E.A.T. students. You're all N.O.T. students. That's N-O-T, not ... *not*. Umm ... Can anyone tell me what N-O-T means?"

Most students were already daydreaming and longing for lunchtime. Those that weren't shuffled, and their eyes shifted sideways as if searching for the one with enough courage to answer. That person was not present.

"Okay then," Maka sighed. "N.O.T. stands for Normally Overcome Target, and it's the basic qualification offered here at DWMA. Over the next year, you're going to learn about Demon Weapons and meisters, the different genetic factors that give us these abilities, and how to harness them."

Every pair of eyes glazed over.

Maka fumed, *I am going to kill Soul!*

Her eyes darted around. Already she felt like she'd been there for hours, but her watch only read nine-oh-three. Hoping that her watch was slow, she looked to the clock above the door to confirm. A much more welcome sight passed within her gaze: Tsubaki, sauntering down the hall.

"Ah! Here we are," she exclaimed as she scrambled to the door, grabbed the taller girl by the arm, and yanked her in front of the class.

Tsubaki mewled as she stood in front of the class. Her skin broke out in goosebumps under the penetrating gaze of thirty N.O.T. students. She jumped as Maka bellowed, "Well, why don't you introduce yourself to the students?"

The blonde's smile seemed friendly, but her eyes roared, "Do something or suffer!"

"I ... ah! I'm T-Tsubaki N-Nakatsukasa," exclaimed the flustered girl. She bent rigidly. "Nice to meet you all!"

Maka smiled to the class. "Tsubaki is a Demon Weapon, and she'll be helping me with my demonstration today."

Tsubaki squeaked with embarrassment and veered toward the door. Maka struggled to keep her in place with her vice-grip, and put the class on hold as she followed the fretful girl into the corridor.

"I can't do a demonstration," shouted Tsubaki in a whisper.

"I'm sorry, but Soul was supposed to help out," replied Maka.

"I'm not even supposed to be here!" replied Tsubaki. "I'm not a teacher. I was just looking for Black-Star. Do you know where he is?"

Maka rolled her eyes. "Probably with Soul. He trashed our apartment earlier, then he and Soul ran off together. Something about a truck's mother or somewhat."

Tsubaki looked like a bride left at the altar. Her lower lip started to tremble, and Maka's irate face softened. She gripped Tsubaki's hand and cooed, "Tsubaki, sweetie, what's the matter?"

"Today, Black-Star told me he was going to be Soul's meister," Tsubaki stammered. "He's gone and dumped me and now he and Soul are going to elope!"

While Tsubaki's started to sob, Maka's face darkened. Before the sobbing could reach full-blown crying, Maka reached up and flicked Tsubaki on the forehead. Then she took hold of the girl's cheeks and wrenched her down to her level. She slowly whispered, "Tsubaki, Soul and Black-Star are not gay together. That's just *your* creepy fantasy. Black-Star can't be Soul's meister. They're just out goofing off somewhere. Understand?"

Tsubaki pursed her lips as her eyes fixated on Maka's.

The blonde's words penetrated her mind and calmed her nerves. Her red eyes stopped leaking and she sniffed back the long trail of snot crawling down her lip. She sighed and nodded resolutely.

"Good," huffed Maka. "Now, let's go do the demonstration."

Tsubaki waved her hand. "Actually, I have to be –"

"Now!" snapped Maka, and Tsubaki followed like a puppy. They strode up to the class that had grown restless with boredom and Maka quieted them down. "Alright, class. We're going to do a demonstration of a Demon Weapon."

Tsubaki closed her eyes, and her body disintegrated into a helical stream of energy. It snaked through Maka's right hand, around her back, and into her left. When the light cleared, Maka held two sickles bound by a chain.

That got the kids' attention, and they clapped excitedly.

"This is Tsubaki's weapon form," said Maka. Her confidence rose despite the pins and needles in her hands where they touched the chain-sickles. She huffed to push the sensation away and focused on the class. "What you need to know about Demon Weapons is that they retain their consciousness while in weapon form. Tell them, Tsubaki."

The children squeaked as they heard Tsubaki's voice emanate from the chain-sickle.

"It's true," said the weapon. "I can hear, see, feel, even smell. Maka's wearing some nice perfume today."

The students stared, dumbstruck. A few even caught a glimpse of the girl's face, reflected in the blades. Some were disturbed while most were absolutely amazed. Even the boy in the 'bazinga' shirt loved the sight.

Maka went on, "But because of that, you have to remember that the weapon is a person too. And they need respect. Weapon and meister need to recognise each other's boundaries." She relaxed her grip around the sickle handles, and they spun freely in her palms. She eyed the class with a grin and said, "Once that is learned, the weapon and meister are one."

Suddenly, she released one of the sickles, and it flew about her body on its own. Maka leapt into the air. Relishing the startled gasps of the class, she flipped, caught the ballistic sickle, and landed on her feet. The amazed children applauded initially, then started to chortle when they saw the chain was wrapped tightly around Maka's waist.

Maka grimaced and her cheeks reddened.

"Of course," she stammered amid the class's chuckles. "You have to be really familiar with each other to do really cool stuff like that." She allowed herself a giggle as she untangled herself. Tsubaki returned to her human form and smiled gauchely.

Once Maka had sobered, she asked, "Any questions?"

Hands shot into the air, and the sight made both the teachers really happy. Maka picked out one of the students, who eagerly asked, "You say that you have to be familiar with each other? What does that mean?"

Tsubaki suddenly burst into a ramble. "Oh, it doesn't mean that we're in a relationship or anything. It just means that we have to have worked together long enough and know each other's bodies ... I mean! I ... uh ..." The kids giggled even more while Maka planted her face into her hand.

"What Tsubaki is trying to say is that you have to have practiced with your partner a lot," said Maka. "It's like a dance between the meister and the weapon. You can't just meet someone, decide to dance, then think you can win a competition, right?"

"Who's the one you practice with, Miss Albarn?" another kid interjected.

Maka cringed. The question brought to mind the nightmare of an idiot that was her roommate. She tried to suppress her resurgent desire to maim her friend and said, "He sick today, so —"

Suddenly, there was a loud crash outside. The startled kids swivelled to look out the window, and one of the kids bellowed, "There's someone shooting up the castle gate!"

Maka raced to the window. Her keen meister eyesight caught the unmistakable yellow and black of her weapon partner's jacket. The sunlight glimmered off the surface of the scythe-blade protruding from where his arm should start. She could hardly see the gunslinger with whom he was fighting, but had a hunch about who it was.

With an irritated tone she could no longer hide, she grumbled, "That there is my weapon partner, and I'm going to force-feed him his own scythe-blade."

# 5 | Grudge Match

Soul's crimson eyes scanned the horizon. His brow was knitted tightly – a show of determination to win the imminent confrontation. He scratched the thinning knee of his magenta trousers and thrust his hand back into the pocket of his yellow jacket. Aside from those odd itches, only one thing kept him from his vigil at the front gates of DWMA.

That thing stood atop the skull sculpture and bellowed, "Pah! This mutha-trucka ain't man 'nough to face God himself!"

*Shaddup, ya dumbass,* thought Soul. His red orbs darted in Black-Star's direction, as the boisterous ninja danced atop the skull.

"He could sense me a mile away," roared Black-Star. "He ran scared, he did!"

Soul heard footsteps, barely audible over his friend's bluster. A slender, black-clad figure stood at the top of the steps of DWMA, two identically dressed girls either side of him. Being a hips man, Soul found himself a tad distracted by the taller girl to the left. The girl on the other side, though seemingly more mature in terms of physicality, was clearly the less mentally developed one. She pointed up at Black-Star and giggled hysterically.

"Kiddo! Ain't that clown funny?" she chortled.

"I ain't no clown!" roared Black-Star. "I am the greatest

meister in the history of meister-dom! I am the God of
this world, and every other world! I am the powerful, the
pleasurable, the indestructible –"

Soul heard a shriek. He looked up and saw Black-Star
tumble down the skull's smooth side. He palmed his face
as his friend rolled down the edge of the sculpture with the
most uncool wails. Luckily, Black-Star managed to land on
both feet, and come out unscathed.

With a manic flourish, the boy roared, "I am the
ultimate Black-Star!" The boy froze, mid-pose, as if
enjoying the fanfare in his head.

Soul harrumphed, and turned to the trio. He still had
his hands in his pockets, as per his code of coolness. And
yet, he felt like he should be worried by how the girls
edged away from the pale, black-clad boy between them.
He had hunched over, and his entire body trembled.

"What is the meaning of this?" growled the boy.

"What's the meanin'?" spat Soul, ignoring his silent, yet
better judgement. "Y'all sniped a mission on Lord Reaper's
wall, what we'd our eyes on."

His companion snarled, "Bein' in Daddy's pocket so ya
can take on a necromancer? No one, not even Death The
Kid, steals from Black-Star, mutha-trucka!"

Death The Kid remained hunched. His body quaked,
and he growled, "How *dare* you lie in wait? How dare you
sully my father's castle?" His yellow eyes shot the most
vividly enraged glare at Soul and Black-Star. He thrust a
shaking finger at the skull sculpture and screamed, "You
cretins shifted that skull two-point-four-eight-nine-three-
two microns to the left!"

Soul's jaw dropped. "What?"

"Don't you dare deny it!" screamed Death The Kid.
Beside him, the short girl fell on the ground laughing,
while the tall girl just shook her head.

"Pah! Of course, I did!" spat Black-Star, his dukes up
and ready. "Consider it part one of operation 'Payback's-a-
bitch!' And now that you're demoralised –"

The tall girl interjected, "Oh, you haven't demoralised anything." Her lips issued a warning, but her eyes glimmered with cockiness.

"Liz, Patty! Transform!" snarled Death The Kid.

The girls' bodies flashed white and dematerialised into guns in Death The Kid's hands. He aimed them at the offenders. Black-Star darted aside with lightning speed. Soul transformed his forearm into a scythe-blade and swiftly deflected the energy beams that burst from the handguns.

Death The Kid harrumphed, "Well, you two have skill, I suppose."

"Skill? You're a cheater!" snapped Black-Star. "Why do you get two weapon partners, damn it?"

"Dude, it ain't screwin' rules to have two weapons," said Soul, his eyes locked on the gunman. "If ya showed up to class, ya'd know that."

"Pah! Class ain't for Gods!" spat Black-Star. "Let's take on this silver-spoonie!"

"Word to that!" returned Soul.

Soul took point and charged Death The Kid. He managed to swat the gun shots aside, while Black-Star charged in his wake. Soul leapt over Death The Kid, distracting him with a kick to the face. His opponent blocked the blow, but didn't notice Black-Star. The ninja came within arms-length, pressed his fists to the gunman's back, and roared, "Black-Star, Big Wave!"

At the last instant, Death The Kid swivelled, crossed his arms over his chest, and blocked the ethereal wavefront that burst from Black-Star's soul. The air around them sizzled with electricity that Death The Kid was only barely able to withstand. He grunted under the force of Black-Star's attack, and retaliated with a barrage of gun blasts. The ninja back-flipped away to gain some ground, dodging the shots that chipped the concrete beneath him.

Soul took the chance and swiped at Death The Kid's

neck. The gunman ducked, and swivelled to counter. Soul put his foot into the gunman's gut, launching him across the plaza toward Black-Star, who readied another mental blast.

Suddenly, Death The Kid tapped the ground, allowing him to pitch mid-air. He locked his legs around Black-Star's neck, flipped, and sent the flabbergasted boy head over heels. Soul leapt through the air and brought his scythe-arm down on the gunman's head. Death The Kid parried the blow with the barrel of one gun, and shoved the other against Soul's solar plexus.

A wave of panic overcame the scythe. The gun went off, and Soul felt the wind escape him like a volcanic eruption. He hit the ground with a deafening thud.

"Goddammit, that hurt!" he squealed. His hands scoured his body, searching for the bullet hole.

"Don't bother," murmured the gun in Death The Kid's left hand. "We don't fire bullets, just bolts of Kiddo's soul wavelength."

"It's enough to neutralise an Asura Egg at ten yards," growled Death The Kid.

The pitter-patter of feet filled the plaza. The combatants looked to the entrance of the castle and saw a horde of young teens. Expressions ranging from perturbed to excited were shot their way. Among the crowd were a few adults, including a blonde girl with pigtails and a taller Japanese girl with a knitted brow.

"Soul, what the Hell?" growled Maka, unable to care that kids were within ear reach.

"This a-hole stole our mission to Egypt," barked Soul as he rubbed his chest. "If it ain't for him, we'd've gotten our hundred souls back."

"Screw that, Soul," snapped Black-Star. "*I'd* have been the one with the souls!"

"What, and you ain't sharin'?" yelled Soul.

"Shut up! Both of you!" roared Maka. "We've got students here, and they'll be looking up to us. Look at what kind of example you're setting!"

Soul and Black-Star eyed the crowd. They took note of every single expression they could see. Black-Star saw the few interested grins amid the rabble, and exclaimed, "I'm sure I'm setting an amazing example! I am a God, after all!"

His albino counterpart was much more reserved. His grin widened, however, when he realised the looks of excitement were directed at his scythe-arm. He turned to Maka and said, "Looks like they're gettin' a damn good example right here. Oi! Kids! Ya better be just as cool as me!"

*BANG!*

Black-Star and Soul hit the ground. Their skulls vibrated like hard-struck tuning forks. Their blurred vision cleared to notice Death The Kid's guns pointed at them. Smoke wafted from the barrels. The plaza erupted with laughter, salting the wounds to their respective egos.

Maka folded her arms and chuckled, "You know what, Soul? Go nuts! Set a good example."

Black-Star shot to his feet and roared, "We'll do more than that, damn it! Soul, let's do it!"

"Word!" returned Soul. He leapt into the air, soaring over Death The Kid toward Black-Star. His body flashed and morphed into his scythe form. With a cocky sneer, Black-Star held out his hands to accept the weapon. The scythe struck his hand, overwhelmed his strength, and pulled him into the ground. His face hit the concrete with a painful crack and a grunt, followed by even more laughter.

"Dude, what the Hell?" exclaimed Soul.

"You're freakin' heavy, Soul!" barked Black-Star as he tried to lift the scythe. His hands started to blister under the strain of the weapon's weight.

"Come on, dude, Maka can lift me fine," returned Soul. The scythe suddenly felt a tremendous force against his spirit, as if a shotgun had hit him. With a flash, he reverted to his human form and kicked Black-Star away. "Quit tryin' to force your wavelength into me!" he yelled.

"Quit bein' a pussy and take it," barked Black-Star.

The boys started to bicker, while Maka just chuckled. She felt a hand tug at her jacket, and saw one of her students.

"I don't get it, Miss Albarn," said the girl. "Why can't the boy pick the scythe up?"

Maka pursed her lips. She quickly scanned the crowd – not with her eyes, but with her soul. She reached out through the aether, sniffing out the scent of every soul within her mind's reach. She huffed with disappointment.

*Another year, and no Grigori Souls,* she thought with a sigh.

To the student, she said, "Remember what I said about how a meister and weapon need to know and respect each other. They need to be compatible." She eyed the gunman, who watched his opponents squabble. She extended the tendrils of her ethereal awareness and felt the three souls before her. She could see the soul of Death The Kid: a rigid entity of deep purple, contrasting with the wispy bright yellow of the two girls that were his handguns.

"Those three," she murmured. "Their souls complement each other. He's clearly got some control issues, but he's also refined and astute, which his weapon partners admire and respect. And those girls, while undisciplined, are adaptive and relaxed." She turned to the student, whose eyes filled with wonder. With a smirk, she eyed the quarrelling married couple nearby. "Those sillies can't even sense each other's presence, much less their souls."

Black-Star's blue-tinted soul erupted with a firework-display of otherworldly sparks and energetic shards. Those explosions grew in ferocity with the volume of his voice. Meanwhile, Soul's fiery red spirit couldn't keep up with its blue rival. It pirouetted around the misfiring bursts of Black-Star's temper and distanced itself, while maintaining an aloof flame of its own.

"Black-Star, I can't do this," he said despairingly.

Black-Star suddenly stopped yelling, and his face softened with worry. "What do you mean?"

"We should break up," said Soul, kicking away a loose stone in the concrete seams. "If we keep going like this, I'll hate you, and I don't want that."

Black-Star clutched his hand over his chest and mumbled, "Well, if that's what you want." His lips trembled. "But, we'll still be friends, right?"

Soul turned yelled, "Of course, we will, dumbass!"

Overjoyed, the two threw their arms around each other. They sobbed and cried cathartically while everyone watched with tremendous confusion. One of the students even asked, "Umm ... are those two gay or something?"

"If only," mumbled a sultry voice. Every single pair of eyes turned to Tsubaki, whose cheeks turned deep red.

Death The Kid harrumphed, "While this is interesting, it's time to end this bout." He twirled his pistols around his fingers, and the air about him simmered with heat. Every current near him came to a standstill, before swirling about his body. The whites of his eyes flashed purple as he and his weapons proclaimed: "Soul Resonance!"

Maka's jaw dropped with excitement. Tsubaki trembled. The hairs on the backs of every student's neck stood on end.

"What's going on?" asked a student.

"Their souls are resonating with each other," Maka explained. As the maelstrom about Death The Kid intensified, so did the searing purple light emanating from his very being. The crowd grew restless with worry, and Maka yelled, "Don't worry, everything's alright."

"What are they doing?" asked another student.

"When meister and weapon resonate, their souls are like standing waves, constructively interfering with each other and raising their combined strength," said Maka. "And with two weapons ..."

She couldn't help but grin at the silly pair, goading

Death The Kid to hit them with his best shot. Black-Star
continued to bluster and taunt. But when those handguns
turned to hand-mounted cannons, Soul grew really
nervous. And when those cannons targeted him and Black-
Star, he bolted out of the way – much to Maka's delight.

Death The Kid's cannons spewed forth a helical beam
of yellow and violet, which struck Black-Star. A grey cloud
concealed the victim from sight. The shocked students
coughed and spluttered as the smoke cleared. Black-Star
lay in a crater, covered in scratches and grit. His twitching
told a worried Tsubaki he still lived, and she pushed
through the crowd toward him.

"Gah! That hurt like a mutha-trucka!" exclaimed Black-
Star when he came to. He glared at Soul. "Bastard! Why
did ya ditch me?"

"Oi! I saw he was gonna kick our asses, so I pulled
out," retorted Soul.

Death The Kid approached them, his weapon partners
in tow. He looked down his nose at his vanquished
opponents.

"You have no means of gauging an enemy," he said to
Black-Star. "There is only so long that such an
understanding weapon partner can protect you from
yourself."

"Screw you, rich boy!" barked Black-Star.
Unfortunately, his muscles were too weak for him to do
anything more than hobble. "I'm Black-Star, damn it!"

Death The Kid ignored the defeated wretch and glared
at the deserter. "You recognise too late when you face a
superior opponent, and abandon your ally at the last
moment," he snapped.

Soul grit his teeth furiously, but could not find any
retort. Maka only made it worse when she said, "You got
that right."

Death The Kid turned to see the pig-tailed meister. He
looked her up and down, and his brow softened only
slightly.

"You at least have some skill to you, Miss Albarn," he rasped. "That said, you fail as a meister if you allow your weapon to fight alone." Maka shivered with indignation and shuffled irately. Her nerves heightened as Death The Kid added, "Your father's praise may be misplaced."

Before any of them could retort, Death The Kid marched toward the entrance to the castle. He turned on his feet and addressed them.

"Although I wish I could ask for better, you are the ones my father has offered," he said with a businesslike tone. "You will come with me to the briefing." Then, he and his weapons walked away.

Maka, Soul, and Black-Star sat flabbergasted. Their gazes darted to one another and they stammered. Only Tsubaki had the presence of mind to ask, "What briefing?"

Death The Kid and his weapon partners looked over their shoulders. In unison, they said, "A mission concerning the future of DWMA."

# 6 | Kiddo's Mission

The white-painted corridor echoed with the sounds of footsteps. The noise rattled the pictures and paintings adorning the bare walls between grey-stone arches. The candles, supported on metal wall-mounted holders, shuddered at the breath of the seven figures, who waltzed toward the red door at the end of the corridor.

Black-Star trudged along, supported by a cheery-faced Tsubaki. Soul and Maka walked a bit ahead of them, though they put a wide berth between each other. Leading the way was Death The Kid and his two identically-dressed weapons.

Soul was the first to speak.

"So you're him they call Death The Kid," he intoned.

"Indeed," said the man in black.

"The one-and-only son of Lord Reaper," said Liz over her shoulder. She had a smile that just screamed pride.

"But it's okay to call him 'Kiddo,'" chirped Patty.

"Ha, as in Beatrix Kiddo[4]?" chortled Soul. Maka sighed while Black-Star managed a weak chuckle.

Kiddo stopped in his tracks, swivelled and snarled, "Tarantino is a hack! I'll not be associated with him!"

Black-Star gathered his strength and pulled away from

---

[4]    The lead protagonist in *Kill Bill*, directed by Quentin Tarantino.

Tsubaki. He caught up to Kiddo and belched, "Why're you associatin' ya self with us, then?"

"Father told me you four are the best of DWMA," said Kiddo. "I'm inclined to disagree, but you're what's available to me."

"Available for what?" asked Maka.

"You shall see soon enough," replied Kiddo.

The group reached the red door. It was a massive rendition of Rodin's *Gates of Hell*, though a sculpture of the DWMA skull trademark sat where the Thinking Man should have been. It's technicolour appearance almost made the demonic artwork inviting.

Kiddo touched his finger to the seam between the two doors, and they flew inwards. A soft flood of wind and smoke buffeted them as the doors revealed the chamber of the Reaper. Kiddo and his weapons marched onto the white carpet, through the forest of black crucifixes, toward the dais in the middle of the dome-shaped chamber.

Maka shuddered slightly as she made her way across the room. She could hardly remember the last time she'd been invited to the Reaper's chamber. Her excitement elevated her out of her earlier irritation with Soul's idiocy.

Black-Star held a confident stance as he plonked along the path to the dais. He acted as if the crucifixes were waving at him as he past, and he bowed with many a cocky chuckle. Tsubaki smiled at his antics, though her eyes begged him silently to calm down.

They reached the dais, and Kiddo turned to the large standing mirror. The mirror's glimmering surface started to heave like boiling water. A black entity burst from the liquid, slithered through the air like a snake, and hit the ground before the mirror. The creature took the shape of a slender being in a long, flowing black cloak. A skull mask concealed his face, but not his expression as two large white hands stuck out from under his cloak and spread wide.

"Welcome! Welcome!" exclaimed the entity.

"'Allo, 'allo, Lord Reaper," chirped Maka with a smile.

The Reaper's lidless black eyes turned to her and he cried, "Maka, you magnificent Madame! Get your scythe-swinging butt over here and give me a hug!"

Maka grinned, and walked forward to throw her arms around the much taller Reaper's body. The white hands enveloped her warmly and the Reaper growled, "It's been too long. How the heck are you?"

"Pissy," muttered Soul.

The Reaper stifled Maka's knee-jerk retort and said, "Soul Eater! Good to see you too. I see you haven't lost your penchant for ticking your meister off."

"Oh, how could I disappoint ya, Reaper?" replied Soul.

The Reaper turned back to Maka and said, "You'll notice Spirit's not here. I was afraid you wouldn't come otherwise."

Maka waved him off. "Don't be silly, Reaper. Getting to catch up would be worth dealing with Papa."

The Reaper tussled her hair warmly, and then turned to Tsubaki and Black-Star. "Tsubaki, my most favourite patient girl. You're doing an excellent job with Black-Star."

Tsubaki's skin prickled with elation and she bowed. "Thank you, Lord Reaper. You're too kind."

"I hope you've been behaving yourself, Black-Star," said the Reaper sternly as he eyed the boy's roughed-up appearance.

Black-Star folded his arms and scoffed, "Ya stupid spawn Kiddo there's what banged me up!"

The Reaper's eyes narrowed, and chills ran down Maka, Soul, and Tsubaki's spines. Black-Star held his chin high as the Reaper turned to Kiddo and muttered, "He can be brash, can't he?"

Everyone let out a relieved sigh, except for Kiddo.

"Father! Could you be serious, please?" he groaned.

The Reaper chuckled and petted Kiddo, earning his son's chiding and growls. Soul and Black-Star snickered at the Reaper's son fretting about the symmetry of his hair.

Maka was less inclined to let the show go on and loudly cleared her throat.

"Lord Reaper, I believe we were summoned for a reason?" she said.

"Right you are, M'lady Maka!" said the Reaper. He stepped back and gestured Kiddo to speak.

Kiddo straightened out his suit and addressed the group.

"A month ago, my weapons and I undertook a mission in Egypt," he began. He ignored the annoyed grunts from Black-Star and Soul. "Intel had indicated a necromancer robbing graves. However ..." He held up his hand, and a table materialised in front of him. Four folders rested atop it, and he gestured them to take one each and read them. "There were at least three Demon Weapons among the grave robbers, and it seems the purported necromancer himself was one as well."

As she flipped through her folder's contents, Tsubaki suddenly blurted, "Oh no!" She mewled sheepishly at everyone's glances and brandished a photo from the folder: a man with intricate tattoos leading from his forehead down to his neck. Everyone else checked their own copies, but gave bemused expressions. "I just recognised those tattoos. I read about a Demon Weapon named Masamune who had them on his face."

The Reaper giggled, "He's been on my radar for a while. Isn't an Asura Egg yet, but ... ooooh boy! He's teetering!"

Tsubaki's jaw tightened slightly with worry. She eyed the picture again. "But this man isn't Masamune. He's too young."

"But Masamune's weapon form was the Uncanny Sword, was it not?" said the Reaper. "With that, he could manipulate the souls of others."

"Do you think he's the necromancer?" asked Tsubaki.

"Not the one I encountered," said Kiddo. "The one I encountered in Egypt was powerful enough to release

Nitocris, the larval Old One."

"That narco-manager was a scary one! Right, Sis?" exclaimed Patty. Beside her, Liz shuddered at the traumatic visions.

"But!" Kiddo interrupted. "What was most concerning was his identity. Check the one I marked in blue."

The group flipped through their files to the picture in question. It belonged to a student record from DWMA.

"He was a N.O.T. student?" blurted Maka bewildered. "And he wasn't registered as having magical powers beyond the DW-666 gene."

"Exactly, Miss Albarn," said Kiddo. "In fact, all the individuals I encountered raiding the tomb in Egypt were N.O.T. graduates. They'd never received combat or magical training. And they were all reported missing by public authorities between three and four months ago."

Kiddo paused to let the information sink in. He eyed the expressions of all the individuals. Maka was clearly on the ball, by the way her green eyes fixated on her file. Soul's red orbs were doing their best to keep focus, but had clearly missed the implications. Tsubaki hadn't pulled her worried gaze from the photo of Masamune, while Black-Star was sleeping with his eyes open.

"Each of the raiders had an identical wound, resembling a sting," said Kiddo. "I didn't have a chance to analyse them, but they may be a signature of some kind of mind control. Based on the personalities of these former students, I don't believe they were acting by their own volition. I believe they have been brainwashed or otherwise manipulated."

"By who?" asked Soul.

"It's *whom*," chided Maka.

"Oh, Jesus, Maka!" growled Soul.

"I don't know," interjected Kiddo. "All I know is that someone is trying to make a Demon Weapon army. There are many more N.O.T. graduates than E.A.T.s, and they're not nearly as well protected as E.A.T.s. They would be easy targets."

"So," Tsubaki stammered. "You want to find who's controlling them."

Kiddo nodded.

"As y'all have probably figured, we think Masamune might be behind it," said the Reaper. "Part of his Demon Weapon ability was mind control. So he's the first suspect."

"Our intelligence indicates Masamune's main force is hiding in Los Angeles," said Kiddo. "Individuals matching the description of several missing N.O.T. graduates have been sighted around a warehouse on Terminal Island. We believe they may be gathering material for a large-scale necromancy experiment."

Maka's eyes gleamed. "And that's why you need us."

Soul and Black-Star shot her a confused glance.

"Isn't it obvious?" asked Maka. "One meister and his weapons against a whole lot of Demon Weapons under the control of a borderline Asura Egg. No offence, Kiddo, but even the son of the Reaper would have his hands full."

Kiddo shook his head. "None taken at all, Miss Albarn. I've asked you here because I will need help to take them down."

The group exchanged glances.

Black-Star quickly puffed out his chest and blurted, "Pah! That kinda crap'd be nothing for a God like me. I could handle it with my bare hands." The people around him rolled their eyes. He quickly added, "But ... with a team, it'd be a sure win." He grinned. "So count me in!"

"I will also join," stammered Tsubaki with a low bow.

Soul gave Maka a shrug. "Might be fun."

"Then we'll join too, Death The Kid," said Maka with a resolute nod.

Kiddo huffed with excitement. He eyed his new recruits, a twinge of apprehension tugging slightly at his heart. He pushed it aside and proclaimed, "Excellent. A team of seven should be plenty to put a stop to this monster." He suddenly broke out in sweat, and his yellow orbs dilated. Within seconds, he was on the verge of vomiting.

"Dude, what's the matter?" asked Black-Star.

"Seven!" cried Kiddo, filled with dread.

"What's wrong with seven?" asked Maka.

Kiddo glared at her, his eyes wide with terror. "Don't you understand, silly girl? Seven's symmetry is terrible! Not only is it an odd number, but its Hindu-Arabic numeral is not symmetrical, whether you cut it horizontal or vertical! No! I can't have this!"

Liz veered toward her meister to calm him, but she was too late. Kiddo fell to his knees and cried, "I need one more! One more! We must make eight! Eight is even, and vertical and horizontal cuts are identical! It is the perfect symmetry!" He turned to the Reaper. "Father! You must join too!"

"No can do's ville, Kiddo-boy," replied the Reaper.

With a wail, Kiddo fell into a foetal position, writhing and punching the floor. Patty couldn't help but laugh at the whole fiasco while her big sister did what she could to calm the boy. The other four just stared incredulously at the 'legendary' son of the Reaper.

"I vote Maka being the leader of this team," intoned Soul.

Tsubaki and Black-Star's hands shot into the air. "Agreed!"

Maka shrieked, "Eh! No way!" She looked to the Reaper and cried, "What's wrong with your son, Lord Reaper?"

"Ha, he's just got a touch of the OCD," chuckled the Reaper. He looked at the bewildered quartet and shrugged, "If only hunting Asura Eggs was as easy as writing their names down. But dealing with quirky people at DWMA? It's an occupational hazard!"

# 7 | Immortal

Kiddo and Black-Star paced the mirrored atrium of DWMA. Black-Star was restless, and periodically stopped walking to engage in fisticuffs with the air. Kiddo, on the other hand, grew more irritated with every tick of the identical watches on each of his hands.

"I'm gonna get 'em," chanted Black-Star as he punched an absent foe. "I'm a gonna snag me some Masamune!"

Tsubaki mewled nearby. "He might not be there, Black-Star. This is only reconnaissance."

"Ain't ya been listenin', Tsubaki?" scoffed Black-Star. "That mo-fo's gonna be there, and we gonna snag us one powerful soul. Your God ordains it so!"

Liz clicked her tongue facetiously and fawned, "Oww, you've got a crush on yourself. Fair warning: the guy you're in love with is a douche."

Black-Star crossed his arms and snorted. Then he swivelled and went back to his boxing practice. Grunts punctuated his every thrust and swipe. Patty's cheeks turned red as she leaned to her older sister and giggled, "He doesn't know you were dissing him!"

The sisters snapped to attention when they heard their meister growl, "Where are they?"

Tsubaki tried a few times to call the tardy pair, but only green speech bubbles lined the right-hand side of her phone's screen. The latest one read, "Hurry up kiddo mad

:-S"

Finally, the sound of footsteps graced their ears. Maka sauntered down the stairs, her long black jacket wafting behind her. Close behind was Soul, and his red eyes radiated ire. He appeared to have a slight limp to his left, which he favoured as he approached the group.

"Sorry we're late," said Maka, bowing low to Kiddo. "Soul made a fuss."

"*I* made a fuss?" exclaimed Soul. "Bitch, I tripped over your Goddamn books and hurt my ankle!"

Maka maintained a wide smile, though her brows twitched with fury. She intoned, "Yes, we are ready to commence the mission."

"And you get in my face over my messiness," Soul growled under his breath.

"Very well," snapped Kiddo. He rubbed his temples in an effort to banish his headache, but it had little effect. He turned to the others. "This is a recon mission. However, if we identify Masamune, we are to apprehend him. Understood?"

"Yes, Kiddo," said Tsubaki.

"Gotcha," said Black-Star with a thumbs up.

"Understood," said Maka.

Soul just grunted.

Kiddo snapped his fingers and the mirror to their left flashed with white light. The team stepped through the portal and instantly felt a blanket of balmy air strike them. A strong cocktail of oil, rusted metal, and salt water filled their noses. Black-Star was quickest to notice the shifting balance of the ground beneath them.

"We're on a boat," he exclaimed.

"Of course, we are," retorted Kiddo. "Specifically, a cargo freighter." With a wave of his arm, the white portal faded into a reflection of himself in the middle of a wooden frame. He eyed the other half of the cardboard box unceremoniously sandwiched between his feet and a slab of shipping container wall. While Liz yawned, Patty excitedly giggled, "We wrecked someone's mirror! Wrecked mirror!"

Maka gave a worried moan at the hole they'd left in the blue shipping container. "Umm … Aren't we supposed to avoid these kinds of leaks?"

"It was necessary," said Kiddo as he beckoned the group away from the mirror and through the maze of cargo boxes. "Unfortunately, that mirror was the closest one to our destination. If you two hadn't been tardy, we could have entered through a more discrete location."

"Maka's fault," quipped Soul.

"Oi! How is it my fault if you're a klutz?" snapped Maka.

As the pair bickered, Liz growled, "Shut up, will you? We'll get caught!"

"Hey!" screamed a crane operator above them.

They looked up in panic to see a flurry of confused dockworkers gazing down at them from the maintenance bridges above. Kiddo noticed one of the workers edging his hand toward an alarm button. Without a command, Liz and Patty transformed into guns, and Kiddo shot a bullet into the man's head, knocking him out. He fired another at the alarm button and destroyed it.

Black-Star heard movement behind them, and saw a few more workers. He saw the panic in their eyes and knew they suspected the worst. The ninja within him took the reins of his manic brain, and he turned to Tsubaki.

"Flashbomb form!" he snapped.

Tsubaki sharply inhaled and exploded in a white flash. A cloud of smoke flooded through the maze of crates, and an epidemic of coughs and splutters spread across the freighter's deck. When the smog lifted, the intruders were gone. The disoriented workers searched, but came up empty. Only when someone saw the steel cut out from a wall of a crate were the police called.

The intruders were far away by then.

Soul and Maka slumped against a stack of unloaded

shipping crates, out of sight of any cameras or dockworkers. Black-Star supported Tsubaki with one arm and mumbled, "You all right, partner?"

"Yeah," panted Tsubaki. "That form just takes a bit out of me."

Kiddo glanced at them and intoned, "I'm seriously regretting my decision."

"Oww, don't be mean, Kiddo," chirped Patty's gun form. "Su-bah-kee did her best."

Maka stood erect and said, "Let's just get this job done. Kiddo, where is the target?"

"There's a warehouse down south, right before the correctional facility," said Kiddo, pointing with Liz' barrel. "We think they're loading supplies smuggled on the freighters." He glared at the four. "Listen, from now on, we need to be as discrete as possible. Stealth is symmetrical."

"Understood," said Maka while Soul groaned.

Black-Star eyed Tsubaki and said, "Ninja sword mode."

"Got it!" replied Tsubaki. Her body flashed and shrunk into a short blade in Black-Star's hand. He twirled it around and whispered, "Stealth mode, active!"

It was hardly stealthy. Black-Star immediately whipped into a flurry of movement. He loudly banged his back against crates, walls, and fences as he darted ahead of the others. Kiddo and Maka could hear his humming of the theme from *Beverly Hills Cop*, and face-palmed in unison.

"Maka, I'll transform," mumbled Soul, unable to support his bro's stupidity this time. As his scythe form materialised in Maka's hands, his voice echoed from the blade, "It's easier to not cringe in this form, anyway."

"Does Black-Star have some kind of mental disorder?" asked Kiddo.

The eye on Soul's scythe form darted in Kiddo's direction, as did Maka's. If Liz and Patty's weapon forms had eyes, they have looked too.

"Seriously?" they all droned.

The two meisters broke into a sprint down the road. They quickly caught up to Black-Star, who had left a trail of unconscious bodies in his wake. Maka cringed as she grabbed the hyperactive ninja by the ear.

"What is wrong with you?" growled the blonde.

"I'm in stealth mode, dammit," retorted Black-Star. "It's not my fault I'm too big and Godly to not notice!"

"It would be easier if you just calmed down," said Tsubaki.

A bit further down the road, a man saw them and yelled, "Hey, what're you kids up to?" In the next instant, he was on the ground, knocked out cold by Kiddo's gunshot.

The son of the Reaper nodded in the direction of a building of white corrugated iron. The words 'Southwest Marine' marked the side of the building in big blue letters. Maka reached out with her mind and sensed dozens of souls meandering about the buildings beyond. They were all Demon Weapons, to be sure, but their souls seemed tainted, as if they were tigers on leashes. One soul stood out in particular. She could see it, standing on a precipice over the ethereal landscape. A sea of chaos writhed below the soul, just itching to receive it.

"I guess this is the place," she said. "I can sense one soul in there, and it looks like how you described Masamune."

Kiddo didn't get a single word out before Black-Star bellowed, "Yahoo! Let's do it, mutha-truckas!"

He leapt over the wire fence in a single bound and sprinted toward the building. Tsubaki didn't bother trying to reason with him, and matched the frantic pace of her meister's soul. He reached the outer building wall, and noted two sentries scaling the fire escape.

"Chain-scythe mode," he growled. Tsubaki complied, and Black-Star jammed the blades into the rusted wall. As if Roadrunner had taken up ice-climbing, Black-Star scaled the wall beside the fire escape, and reached the sentries before they heard his deafening yells.

He brought his foot against the nearest one, knocking him down the stairs. Then he landed before the other, whose arm swiftly morphed into a mace head. Black-Star dodged the first blow, and crossed Tsubaki's chain-scythes to parry the next. He swiftly kicked the sentry's knees out and head-butted him square on the nose. The other dazed sentry reached for his radio. Black-Star promptly threw one of the chain-scythes, the interconnecting chain lengthening to reach the radio and demolish it. The scythe blade wound around the man's neck and came back into Black-Star's waiting hand. He pulled hard, yanking the man's head right into his knee.

The sentries fell still.

Kiddo swooped in on his hover board to find Black-Star posing over his vanquished opponents.

"Are you kidding me?" he scream-whispered.

"I handled the guards," retorted Black-Star. "I wasn't caught."

Down below, a figure emerged from the warehouse and let out a holler. Both Kiddo and Black-Star's hearts skipped beats as the man called out a few more of his comrades. Their arms changed into all manner of weapons, from spears to swords, and they charged for the stairs.

A roar from the road nearby drew their attention, and they saw Maka sprinting toward them. Soul's scythe blade glimmered in the sunlight as Maka spun through the air toward them. She locked blades with a knife-hand, but wasted no time and kicked her opponent's temple with as much force as she could muster. The knife-wielding woman fell to the ground motionless, and a few of her comrades tripped over her. Maka butted an oncoming attacker with Soul's handle, and bludgeoned another with the back of the scythe blade. She pole-vaulted over the rabble of Demon Weapons and took on a mace wielder, who had a tad more skill than his fellow outlaws.

Maka was so preoccupied with the fight, she didn't notice the bald man behind her. With an enraged sneer, the man's hand turned into a pipe that smelled like high-octane petrol. He withdrew a cigarette lighter from his pocket and pointed the pipe at Maka.

Only a few drops of flammable liquid made it out of the pipe's mouth before a metal disk struck the man's head and sent him to the ground. The disk drew an arc in the air around Maka, felling several enemies and distracting the others long enough for the scythe meister to knock them out. The disk came to a stop in Black-Star's hand, revealing itself to be a gigantic blunted shuriken. Tsubaki's reflection looked out from the surface of the shuriken, and her eyes scanned the vicinity.

Maka glanced around, finding no other attackers.

"Looks like we got 'em all," intoned Soul.

"Not yet," said Kiddo as he came to a soft landing on the asphalt. He marched purposefully toward the warehouse entrance. Black-Star and Maka followed closely behind. A few men and women rushed about, loading boxes into a semitrailer bearing the Coca-cola logo. A couple broke off from the job to attack the meisters. Maka and Kiddo took them on, while Black-Star lingered and scanned the warehouse.

"Black-Star, what are you waiting for?" exclaimed Tsubaki, her chain quivering.

"Where's that tattooed mo-fo?" growled Black-Star.

Tsubaki's scythe-blades suddenly shrieked. Her right handle wrenched itself out of Black-Star's hand and flew toward Maka. It intercepted a blow from a woman with a rapier for an arm. Then the chain shortened, and dragged Black-Star into the fray with Maka and Kiddo.

"We need to help our friends, not go ego feeding!" snapped Tsubaki.

Black-Star quickly recovered his footing and parried blows from three mace wielders and a nunchaku user. Yet his mind lingered on finding that extra-juicy Masamune soul. When his gaze wandered, Tsubaki's chain locked onto his chin and dragged him back into the fight.

"Focus!" she snapped.

The handles of her chain-scythe form started to vibrate in Black-Star's hands. He gripped them tighter, but it only made Tsubaki shriek in pain. Frustrated, Black-Star tossed her weapon form into the air, and laid out his four opponents with his bare hands. Then, he looked up to the air-borne chain scythes and focused his thoughts into them. He reached out through the ethereal void toward Tsubaki's soul and murmured, "Tsubaki, now ain't the time to play 'who's boss.' We gotta get this done. Deal?"

Tsubaki stood in the void, shimmering in the beige light of her soul. She cringed irritably at her partner's rigidity and his unwillingness to follow her instruction for once. Yet, she couldn't deny that he was right.

"Deal," she sighed.

Black-Star held out his hands and caught the chain scythe. He looked around at the battle, and grinned cockily. "Tsubaki, let's do it!"

In unison, they roared, "Soul Resonance!"

The air around Black-Star's body shimmered with blue light. It rippled along the chain of Tsubaki's weapon form, and grew brighter as the chain lengthened. It girdled around him, guided by Tsubaki amplifying his energy through the resonance link. Maka and Kiddo gazed in amazement at the boy, whose skill was finally on display. Any opponent near him withdrew anxiously.

Suddenly, Black-Star released one of the scythes, and it shot outward. It snaked its way through the warehouse, mesmerising the onlookers as it whipped by. Then, it was back in Black-Star's hand again, and he felt Tsubaki's soul through the resonance link.

"Trap-Star! Activate!" they roared.

The chain contracted with lightning speed, latching onto limbs and lashing stomachs. The chain sped toward Black-Star like an elastic band, and it caught nearly every remaining enemy in its snake-like grasp. Black-Star stood triumphantly beside the bunch of people, lassoed together like bad-guys in an Old Western.

"Umm ... Black-Star?" stammered Tsubaki. The boy looked at the rabble, and saw Maka and Kiddo, scrunched up in the middle of his catch, and looking really angry.

"Haha! Ain't that funny, eh?" exclaimed Black-Star. "Maybe we need a little more practice!"

"What the Hell is wrong with you?" yelled Kiddo. With a roar, he blasted his soul wavelength through his guns. A burst of purple light threw the rabble of people into the air, and knocked Black-Star off his feet. Tsubaki and Soul retook their human forms and dragged their dazed meisters away from the commotion, while Kiddo tried to shoot down as many of the rogue Demon Weapons as he could.

Outside his vision, one of the enemies reached the semitrailer, revved the engine, and peeled out of the warehouse. A lucky few managed to hitch a ride before the truck had accelerated too much. Those that remained simply raced for the water's edge and dove. They didn't resurface.

"What're they doing?" exclaimed Soul.

"Better to die than be caught," said Maka breathlessly.

Determined to catch them, Kiddo summoned his hover board to his feet and he tried to chase the fleeing vehicle. A figure appeared out of thin air in front of him, and booted him down into the asphalt.

Maka winced as Kiddo hit the ground hard, and looked up to see the figure that had hit him. He was the very same person from the photo. The man's shadow had somehow formed solid tendrils, upon which he stood, as if they were a pair of stilts. His young face was covered in the tattoos of Masamune. Tsubaki saw them, and her heart sank in her chest.

"Such is to be expected from a Multi-Form such as you," said the figure in a deep voice that did not match his physique. His black eyes glared down at Tsubaki. "You still have much to learn. Isn't that right, Immortal?"

*Immortal,* thought Black-Star.

Kiddo leapt to his feet and proclaimed, "Uncanny Sword Masamune. I, Death The Kid, hereby place you under arrest on suspicion of illegal necromancy."

The man slowly descended from the air as his umbral stilts melted into the ground. His bare feet sizzled as they touched the hot asphalt, but he hardly seemed to notice. He approached Kiddo and held his hands out.

"You got me, officer," intoned the boy. "As for Masamune, he sends his apologies."

The tattoos suddenly leapt off his skin and retreated into his shadow, which crawled its way to the shade of the building nearby before snapping back to him like a drawn out spring. The boy collapsed.

"What the Hell?" exclaimed Soul.

"This isn't Masamune," said a disappointed Kiddo. "In addition to manipulating souls, the Uncanny Sword moves through shadows. In all likelihood, the real Masamune was on that truck." He knelt down to inspect the boy. He checked his collar, arms, and chest, but found no white welt.

"This one looks fine, Kiddo," murmured Liz. Her barrel shuddered as she asked, "Was this kid just a puppet?"

"Possibly," replied Kiddo.

"Then, ain't that means the stings ain't what Massive-Moonie uses to, ya know, control folks?" asked Patty.

Kiddo gritted his teeth with frustration.

*Too many Goddamn unknowns,* he inwardly growled.

He turned to the others and said, "This wasn't a wash. We at least have someone we can question."

"Then let's get him back to DWMA," said Maka. She added with an outstretched finger, "Discretely!"

As Soul and Maka moved to pick up the unconscious boy, Black-Star turned to Tsubaki. He finally noticed the upset look on her face. He tentatively extended his resonance link to his weapon, and felt her horror. At that, he got a slight inkling about why Tsubaki had been so controlling during the fight.

But though his simple mind had missed quite a few things that day, there was one thing he had definitely noticed.

*Why did that guy call Tsubaki 'Immortal?'*

## 8 | The Reaper's Tea Party

The Reaper's mirror rippled with a video feed of an interrogation cell, in the catacombs deep beneath Death City. The young man sat at a table, his arms wrapped around him as he shivered nervously. Kiddo sat opposite him with his fingers threaded, and spoke softly to the boy. The sound of their conversation wasn't terribly audible through the Reaper's mirror, which made the shadowy entity sigh with disappointment.

"I shoulda got the surround sound," he moaned. "My fault for being a cheapskate."

Black-Star scoffed, "We don't need no sound to know that brat'll crack. Just gimme a minute with him."

"Black-Star, just let Kiddo handle this," said Tsubaki.

Maka watched the interrogation unfold, while Soul just sat on the steps near the mirror and played on his phone. His phone dinged and he checked the message. Maka caught a glimpse of the nude picture Blaire had just texted him.

"You pig!" she shrieked as her foot connected with his head.

"What the Hell, Maka?" exclaimed Soul, rubbing the back of his head.

"So Blaire is sexting you now?" growled the blonde as she scooped up his phone. "What other lewd nonsense have you got in here?"

Soul lunged for the phone as Maka scanned through his image history. She couldn't dodge and look at the pictures at the same time. Soul grabbed her shoulder, wrested her around, and snatched the phone away.

"Jesus, you psycho!" snapped Soul. "Blaire sends me those pics all the time. But I delete them!"

"Yeah right!" retorted Maka. "You probably just put them in the cloud so that I won't find them!"

The Reaper leaned over and mumbled, "Umm … Could you please be quiet?"

At that, the door to the Reaper's chamber opened, and in waltzed a red-haired man in a grey shirt and suit combination. His relaxed yet lascivious expression turned furious when he saw Maka and Soul fighting.

"Oi! Soul Eater!" roared the man. "What're you doin' with my baby girl?"

Horrified at the sight, Maka face-palmed. She moaned, "Just stay out of this, Papa!"

But the man didn't stay out of it. He charged forward, ignoring the Reaper pleading, "Oh, Spirit. Wait a moment, please."

Spirit grabbed Soul by the scruff of the neck and wrenched him into the air. "You did something bad to my precious Maka, didn't you?"

This was hardly the first time Spirit had manhandled Soul, and the albino had long-since grown tired of it. He aloofly retorted, "Only banging her every night!"

Spirit choked in horror and clenched his fist. He screeched, "You piece of sh–"

A swift karate-chop from the Reaper floored all three of them, and they were silent.

"Shut the heck up, all of you," snapped the Reaper. "It's hard enough to hear this as it is."

The Reaper got his three minutes of silence while the trio rubbed their sore heads. Spirit, having received many such chops before, recovered first. He thrust a finger in Soul's face and softly snarled, "You assaulted my daughter, didn't you? Admit it!"

"Papa, he didn't do anything like that," said Maka.

"Yeah, it was totes consensual," said Soul with a grin and a wink her way.

"Not helping, Soul," growled Maka.

Spirit turned to Maka with a soft expression and said, "It's alright, Maka. I know you'd never go for such a creep like this." He patted her on the head. "I love ya, my baby girl."

The touch and the phrase made Maka's skin crawl. She swatted his hand away and growled, "Just go away and play with your hookers, Papa."

Spirit's face twisted into an agonised countenance and tears burst from his eyes. He suddenly swivelled and raced off, screaming, "My baby girl! Why are you so horrible and selfish to me?"

Both Maka and the Reaper let out the same dejected groan and rubbed their temples. When the latter returned his gaze to the mirror, he saw that the young man was alone in the room. Kiddo had left. The Reaper eyed Maka and Soul, who still bickered nearby. Black-Star boxed with thin air while Tsubaki updated her social media.

*They really should be more focused on their mission,* thought the Reaper. *On the other hand, it's nice that they're so lax.*

His eyeholes narrowed on the image of the jittery man.

*This is odd, though. Masamune is known to kill his hosts before releasing them. Fewer witnesses that way. Why would he leave this one alive? He might've been in a hurry to escape Tsubaki, what with all that hullabaloo about the camellia plants ... Hmm ... Here's hoping, at least.*

The Reaper sensed his son's arrival, and turned from the mirror to greet him. Kiddo's tired eyes radiated frustration, only some of which, the Reaper knew, had to do with the interrogation.

"So, Kiddo, what did he say?" asked Maka.

"He's from a village in Gunma, Japan," said Kiddo. "The last thing he remembers before waking up in that cell was being in his bedroom. He said the shadows in his room started to move and, next he knew, he was sitting in that chair."

"He ain't a Weapon?" asked Soul.

"He doesn't even have any magical abilities," replied Kiddo.

Black-Star spat, "Bullcrap! Clearly, you ain't no int-alligator!"

"Interrogator," said Tsubaki warmly.

"Dun't matter," barked Black-Star. "Gimme a minute with him. *I'll* make him talk."

"No," the Reaper said curtly. He eyed all the meisters and weapons present. "We'll keep him in the cell overnight. Make sure he's properly fed."

"C'mon, Reaper!" exclaimed Black-Star. "My fists demand a fight."

The Reaper's big white hands rose to silence the boisterous ninja. He glared at Black-Star and said, "I want to see what he does. If he's still here tomorrow, we'll see him returned to his family."

"He may be our only lead, Reaper," said Maka.

"Right now, he's useless," said Kiddo. His gaze shot daggers at Black-Star. "I'd like to discuss *your* conduct at the dock!"

"My conduct?" retorted Black-Star. "I had to go in and fight the bad guys. I'm a God! It's obvious that I'd do it!"

"Shut up!" barked Kiddo. "In case you were too busy showing-off, defenceless N.O.T. students are being brainwashed into an army. We don't find out who's doing it and stop them, we're done for. That's why you're here, not so you can compensate for your own insecurities!"

Black-Star sneered, and he drew near to the Reaper's son. He glared into those yellow orbs and snarled, "You shouldn't piss me off, Death. Think of how bad it'd be to be on God's bad side ... then multiply it by a billion. That ain't half as bad as what *I'm* like."

Kiddo was unfazed. He simply returned a bored, tired

stare. He swivelled and marched out of the room. Not another word left his mouth.

Unnerved by the silence, the Reaper clapped his hands together and exclaimed, "Well then, that's it for now. Go and get some rest and be back here tomorrow morning. Then we'll work out what to do with our prisoner. 'Kay?"

Black-Star marched off silently, Tsubaki nervously tiptoeing after. Soul and Maka followed, but the Reaper caught the blonde by the shoulder and said, "Maka Dear, why don't we have a chat? We didn't really get a chance to catch up, did we?"

Maka's smile peeked through the fog of the earlier confrontation, and she chirped, "That'd be good."

Soul casually saluted the Reaper. "I'll be fine not hangin', Reaper. Plus, my turn to cook dinner tonight anyway." And he strutted off, his hands in his pockets and his shoulders bobbing to the beat in his head.

The Reaper snapped his abnormally large cuboid fingers, and a quaint table and chairs appeared between them. Laid out on it was an old tea set, a gentle flow of steam meandering out the spout of the pot. As Maka sat down, her eyes narrowed suspiciously.

"This is the set you and I used for tea parties when I was five," she said.

"I thought it fitting, girlfriend!" quipped the Reaper, in his best impersonation of Barbie (or Miley Cyrus – he was never really sure).

"I used to invite my dollies around too," said Maka after sipping her tea.

"And let's not forget Spirit," intoned the Reaper, much to Maka's dismay. "Remember, he was always your guest of honour."

Maka rolled her eyes. "Seriously, Reaper, I haven't even put jam on a scone."

The Reaper waved her off and took a seat. His mist-like cloak carpeted the ground beneath the seat as he slurped his tea. And yet, despite Maka's attentive gaze fixated upon the rim of his cup, she could not see his lips beneath the mask.

"Honestly, Reaper, how do you do that?" she exclaimed with a vexed chuckle. "Where is your mouth?"

"Behind my mask, my dear," replied the Reaper nonchalantly.

"Do you ever take off the mask?" retorted Maka, though she knew straight away what the answer would be.

"Ha, please," replied the Reaper with a chuckle. He set his teacup down and threaded his fingers together. "So then, how're you faring on the bottom rung?"

"Ugh, don't remind me," growled Maka.

The Reaper just giggled, "How are you not reminded every day? Didn't you invite that magic cat to live with you?"

"We blew up her house thinking she was a Witch," replied Maka. "It was the least I could do, since I wasn't paying attention to what kind of soul she had. In reality, it was Soul's fault. He was pissing me off, constantly checking out Blaire's googly eyes … her shapely hips … her big double-dee boobies!" She almost crushed the teacup in her hands at the thought. With a practiced breath, she brought herself back to the centre. But her persistent bad mood had made that centre a moving target, and she remained riled up.

"Well, Soul and Blaire are getting along?" the Reaper asked as his phantom mouth consumed a marmalade-coated scone.

"Too well," grumbled Maka. "I'm certain they're having showers together when I'm not looking. Soul and I have been together for years, and yet he hardly looks at me in the same way."

"Do you want him to?" asked the Reaper.

Maka's cheeks turned red and she looked away with a cough. She refilled her cup. The teapot clattered with the shaking of her hand.

"Typical men," she snarled. "Throw 'em a pair of titties

and they act like scoundrels."

The Reaper made tongue-clicking sounds and raised his finger. "Maka Dear, you shouldn't generalise. Besides, Soul says he deletes the naughty pictures Blaire sends him. Maybe he doesn't like her advances either."

Maka scoffed, "Of course, a man would defend his fellow men."

"Who ever said I was a man?" said the Reaper pompously.

Maka's jaw dropped and her tea almost slipped out of her hand.

"Umm ... Lord Reaper, are you a woman?" she stammered.

"Nope," replied the Reaper after inhaling another scone.

"Then why did you say you weren't a man?" asked an increasingly-confused Maka.

"I didn't say I wasn't," said the Reaper. "I just asked, 'Who ever said I was a man?' I suppose I let people use the male pronoun because there isn't really a word for what I am in English. Plus ... 'it' just seems too impersonal." He set his cup down and began to pace. "Since I'm not really human, it's easy for me to be neutral. I have no reason to believe Soul is interested in Blaire. And, in my opinion, the only reasons *you* have are those you're looking for. So, Maka Dear, what are those reasons?"

Maka pursed her lips. Her body trembled, her cheeks felt hot, and sweat beaded at her hairline. But the rest of her body felt freezing cold. Her mind filled with the image of a six year old girl with blonde pigtails. That little girl's eyes were filled with confusion, concern, and sadness. The cause of that sadness was a red-haired man waltzing down a street in Paris, a Mademoiselle on each arm.

"Well, Reaper," she said curtly. Tears were near her eyes but she held them back. "Take it from a woman who's lived right in the thick of it. Men are slime." She downed the rest of her tea, ignoring the burning of her throat, and stood up. "Thank you for the tea," she said with a forced smile. She then turned and left the chamber.

If the Reaper had a mouth, he'd have smiled a melancholic smile. He waved his hand and the table vanished. He turned to his mirror and let out a tired sigh.

\* \* \*

Maka and Soul both reached the DWMA castle bright and early. It had been an effort on Soul's part to avoid Blaire's morning *exhibition*. That hadn't totally bridged the wide rift between the weapon and meister, but it at least smoothed things over.

They got quite the surprise when they saw Black-Star and Tsubaki in the Reaper's chamber. Kiddo, Liz, and Patty were there too, grim looks on their wide-awake faces.

"What's goin' on with the kid?" asked Soul.

"Dead," whispered a horrified Tsubaki.

"And the guard we had posted is missing," said Black-Star.

"What happened?" exclaimed Maka. She and Soul raced to the Reaper's mirror, which showed a feed of the boy's cell. Between the trio of Death City CSIs scouring the room, Maka caught a glimpse of the bed. There the young man lay, on his side, a flood of crusted blood oozing from his mouth and from a gaping hole in his solar plexus.

"What the Hell?" exclaimed Soul. "Did a chestburster get him or something?" Maka slapped him over the head. "What? That's what a chestburster looks like!"

"We're not dealing with a fictional creature, Soul," said Kiddo.

The Reaper stepped forward and chimed, "I have the video from the previous night." He twirled his finger, and the video rewound. The young man lay in a restless sleep. He started to rub his stomach. Then scratch it. Then he started to convulse as a tiny thing pushed its way through his skin and shirt. Blood erupted from his mouth and chest as the thing crawled all the way out. The man breathed his horrified last at the sight of a blood-covered scorpion.

"So, chestburster," said a creeped-out Soul.

"Watch," said Black-Star.

The arachnid scurried under the bed upon hearing the door unlock. In barged the cell guard. He approached the corpse with horror, but before he could run to get help, the scorpion leapt out from under the bed and stung his forearm. The man grabbed his wounded arm, and his eyes radiated panic at the wretched creature. He made a move toward the pest, but stopped as his body started to shake.

*Oh God, this better not be another chestburster,* thought Soul.

The guard doubled over slightly, and then stood upright and looked around. The scorpion approached him, and he offered his hand. The creature climbed onto him, and he left the room.

"Wait! Hold that frame!" snapped Kiddo. He pushed Soul and Maka out of the way and swiped at the mirror. The view zoomed in on the man's forearm, revealing a white, veiny welt.

"That's it!" exclaimed Kiddo. "That scorpion creature must be what's controlling the N.O.T. students." He immediately lost himself in his frantic musings. His unfocused yellow eyes darted around aimlessly. He suddenly blurted, "I need to do some research." And in a flash, he and his weapons were out of the room.

Maka, Soul, and Tsubaki wore expressions of concern, disgust, and horror. The sight of that scorpion digging its way out of the man was enough to ensure they never watched an *Alien* movie ever again.

Black-Star, on the other hand, had a brow knitted with annoyance.

"He shoulda just let me at him," he snorted.

The Reaper patted him on the head and said, "While it's grisly, we may have gotten a lead."

* * *

Cold night air scurried through the buildings of downtown Death City. The Moon beat down through the alleyways and illuminated the face of a man with a white, veiny welt on his forearm. His blank stare remained fixed on the woman before him. Her purple braided hair gleamed in the Moonlight. As if controlled by her mind, it flicked and flagellated the silk, backless dress that revealed the scorpio tattoo etched into her skin.

"That is the best way into DWMA?" asked the woman. Her strident voice hardly perturbed the man, who simply nodded. "Excellent," she said. "Now, lay down and stop breathing."

The man did so. The woman gazed down at him as his face turned blue and his extremities started to twitch with discomfort.

"Too long," snapped the woman.

She promptly jammed her stiletto into his chest, and he fell still. She wiped the viscera from her heel with his shirt, and then waved her hands. An army of tiny scorpions scampered out of the sewer drains and coated the man. The woman turned to leave the alleyway.

The corpse vanished before she reached the road.

# 9 | The Scorpion Tattoo

On the third Saturday of each month, there was a bazaar held in the southeast quadrant of Death City. For a small fee, anyone could set up a stall and sell their wares. Mostly you'd see ladies from the Southern States selling homemade jam. But there were also a lot of people from Asia who set up stalls for food and homemade jewellery. Often, there would be at least one stall for every province of India. At one stall, you could get a dosa made by a Tamil lady; next door, a Sikh would fix you a lovely mango lassi; next one after that, you could enjoy chanpuruu from an Okinawan guy whose arm-blade chopped up the vegetables.

It was a great sight to behold. Not to mention, it was also a testament to the Reaper's charm that he could get such a huge diversity of people to happily set-up shop in a place called 'Death City.' But, if you were a Demon Weapon, you'd hardly care about that.

Soul certainly couldn't, as he sat cross-legged on a plastic mat between a Korean kimchi stall and a Finnish busker singing a Hatsune Miku song. A pile of hardcover books sat in front of him with the sign, 'Used Books for Sale!' His broad-brimmed hat guarded him from the intense midday sun, yet he still had an annoyed look. The cause: Maka, seated next to him with an irate scowl.

A short boy, about ten years old, approached the pair.

He leaned down to take one of the books, only to hear Maka's knee-jerk growl. He saw murder in her eyes and ran away shrieking.

"Jesus, Maka!" snapped Soul. "That's the tenth customer you've scared off. We won't get rid of these if you've always got that look."

"This is how my face always looks!" retorted Maka.

"Now *that's* a load of crap," said Soul. "You just don't want to let go of your books."

"Why do we need to sell them so badly?" moaned Maka.

Soul lifted up his bandaged ankle and yelled, "'Cause of this, you dumb bitch! I twisted my ankle tripping over your books. And you never even read them!"

Maka looked away with a scowl. Out the corner of her eye, she saw another boy approach. She heard Soul yell, "Welcome! Please, pick one of these great books!" But before the boy could even respond, Maka shot him a look that said, "Touch it and I'll rip out your spinal column and beat you with it!" The boy fled in fear.

"That does it," said Soul. He grabbed a popsicle stick from the lassi stall nearby and tried to shove it in Maka's mouth, sideways. "Quit struggling, girl! I saw this on *VSauce*. This'll make you happy about getting rid of these stupid books! Come on then!"

Maka smacked him over the head as he tried to push the popsicle stick against the side of her lips. The sight drew the attention and laughter of the customers of the nearby stalls. The laughter grew even more raucous when Maka grabbed one of the heavier books on the pile and clobbered Soul over the head with its thick spine.

A shriek barely made its way through the chortling crowd. Everyone who heard it looked toward the girl near the carousel in the square. But only Maka could sense the abnormal soul at the epicentre of the chaos. She leapt through the crowd, pushing against the people fleeing the scene. She reached the front of the crowd and beheld a sight that made even her want to run screaming.

A girl of Indian descent stood over another girl. Her victim's blood dripped from a butterfly blade that melded into her shoulder. She looked around blank-faced, ignoring the horrified cries of the girls Maka assumed were her friends.

Maka focused on the girl's face, and recognised her as one of her senior N.O.T. students.

"Abhilasha!" she exclaimed. "What are you doing?"

Abhilasha turned lazily and locked eyes with her teacher. Maka gasped in horror when she saw the white, veiny welt on her forearm. The girl charged her, her butterfly blade swinging mindlessly. Soul appeared between Maka and the raging student. His arm morphed into a scythe blade, and blocked the blow.

Maka yelled, "Everyone, back away. Right now!"

One of the girl's friends raced forward and cried, "Abhi! What's wrong with you?"

Abhilasha swivelled wordlessly and sped toward the girl. Soul managed to catch up just in time to parry her blade and kick her into the carousel fence. He turned to the girls and roared, "Run! Now!" Then he turned to Maka and said, "Let's go!"

His body morphed into his scythe form, which Maka raced forward to grab. She locked blades with the girl, but her strength faltered every time she made eye contact with her opponent. She couldn't shake the memories of Abhilasha's first day.

"C'mon, Maka, focus!" growled Soul.

"We can't hurt her, Soul!" cried Maka. She stumbled back as the girl twirled in mid-air, her razor-sharp blade slicing the air with a high-pitched chirp. Maka managed to divert the blade into the ground with enough time to knock their opponent with the butt of Soul's scythe-blade.

The beady eye on Soul's scythe form darted toward the welt on Abhilasha's arm, and Maka heard him gasp.

*Kill a kid at a crowded place and make everyone go nuts,* he thought.

"The brainwasher's around here somewhere!" he intoned.

* * *

Black-Star hadn't wanted to get up that morning. It was a Saturday, which was his day to sleep in.

"A God needs his beauty sleep, dammit!" he growled as he and Tsubaki made their way toward the DWMA castle.

"Yes, but we're on the roster for security today," said Tsubaki, cheerful as ever.

"And why are we on the security roster?" asked Black-Star.

"Because of the breach last week," said Tsubaki.

"I was bein' rhetorical, Tsubaki," grunted Black-Star. "Because we let in a kid with a scorpion in his guts, I now gotta work on a Saturday!" Under his breath, he snarled, "Eff-in' Kiddo and his stupid missions."

The rest of the morning went from infuriatingly dull to depressingly boring. Most of the time, Black-Star just looked longingly at the bazaar in the southeast part of town.

*Gah! I want me some Goddamn Szechuan and some Ramen to wash it down with,* he internally roared.

Of course, it hadn't helped much that Kiddo was two hours late for his shift. When he finally appeared, Tsubaki had to hold Black-Star back for fear the mad ninja would beat Kiddo to death.

"I apologise for my tardiness," said Kiddo calmly amid Black-Star's vengeful yells. "There were necessary preparations that took longer than expected." His identically-dressed weapons straightened out their pink blouses and jeans as he beckoned them to follow to the west wing of the castle.

"Necessary preparations, my ass!" snapped Black-Star as he shook himself free of Tsubaki's hold.

Liz lagged a little and mumbled, "He was straightening

out the pictures in his room. Wore out a tape measure to do it."

Black-Star exploded, "Are you freakin' kidding me!?"

Liz raced down the hall before Black-Star could give chase. With all his remaining energy, all the boy could do was pace. Tsubaki remained vigilant as her meister threw his tantrum. A good fifteen minutes later, Black-Star plonked down next to her with a scowl and watched her play games on her phone.

The wind carried a faint shriek through the open window behind them. Both of them shot up and looked outside. They could see people at the bazaar shrieking and running from something near the carousel.

"Tsubaki, ninja sword mode," said Black-Star as he climbed onto the windowsill.

Tsubaki's sword form materialised in his hand and they matched their hearts' tempos. Black-Star suddenly felt a pull on his shoulder, and turned to see Patty. Her eyes radiated a determined air as she said, "Come with me, now!"

"There's a problem at the bazaar!" protested Black-Star.

"Kiddo says it's distracting," replied Patty as she yanked him down the corridor.

"Distracting?" exclaimed Black-Star. "That shithead thinks helpin' people is distracting?"

Tsubaki chimed in, "I think she means it's a distraction! Kiddo might need our help elsewhere in the castle."

"He does!" shouted Patty.

Black-Star hesitated. He eyed the commotion in the park, and could just make out Soul's scythe blade. With a huff, he followed Patty down the hall. She led him through the corridors of DWMA, down a fire escape on the west-most side, and into the basement of the castle. There, at the end of a candle-lit corridor they found Liz, Kiddo, Spirit, and a group of DWMA meisters, their weapons at the ready. Liz and Patty transformed and Kiddo caught them. He then turned to Black-Star.

"We think the enemy is making their move," he said. With a wave of his hand, the door opened, releasing a rush of stale air. "I'm certain they're going for the west sewer entrance."

"Based on what?" asked Black-Star.

"There's a main pipeline that leads straight up into the castle," said Spirit. "All the others were sealed but we keep that one open for ventilation."

"Perfect access point to bring in an army," Tsubaki concluded.

Kiddo raised his voice. "Squad one, you're with me. We'll block the south tunnel going straight in. Squad two, you're with Spirit. Take the east-facing tunnel, and push them into the central atrium. Black-Star, you have squad three. Block the upper access points for the atrium. We're expecting a lot of brainwashed N.O.T. students, so do not fatally harm them. Understand?"

The group grunted in agreement.

"Move out!" barked Spirit.

The three squads charged down the corridor. Spirit's squadron broke off first and head down a path to the left. Then Kiddo's broke right. Black-Star hardly noticed. His lingering resentment for Kiddo fuelled his legs and his squad couldn't keep up the pace.

"Black-Star, slow down!" snapped Tsubaki.

The crazy ninja yelled over his shoulder, "If ya can't keep up with God, then don't bother comin'!"

Furious, Tsubaki took her chain-scythe form, and dug one of the blades into the ground to slow him. Her chain wrapped around him and dragged him back.

"You need to pay attention," said Tsubaki firmly. "You just missed the turn off to the upper atrium."

Black-Star looked back and saw his squad waiting at the right junction. They shot him confused and concerned looks that just annoyed him. He flicked Tsubaki's other scythe into his hand and raced down the proper path. It took a little more chiding from Tsubaki before he slowed his pace to match his squad.

They reached the upper level of the basement atrium. Black-Star edged his gaze around the corner and looked down into the chamber. He could see Kiddo's shadow at the south entrance, and Spirit's red hair around the corner of the east entrance. The only path was the one coming in from the west. But there was no sound, nor any footprints in the dust carpeting the floor.

Black-Star edged onto the upper level boardwalk, and looked to Kiddo, who had stuck his head around the corner.

"See anything?" he mimed.

"Nope!" yelled Black-Star. His voice echoed through the entire chamber and reverberated down the halls. If Tsubaki hadn't been in weapon form, she'd have face-palmed.

Spirit walked into the middle of the atrium and looked straight down the westward passage. He even shone his flashlight into the tunnel, and then gave a confused shrug.

Suddenly, the Reaper's voice blared through the halls. Full of concern, he yelled, "Get to the vault! Lost contact from the guards there! Go, now!"

"Damn it! This was a diversion too!" growled Kiddo. He looked to Black-Star and Spirit and yelled, "Go!"

The squads flooded into the atrium and followed Kiddo's lead into the southward tunnel, which curved inward. Kiddo darted to the left, and then to the right, before he leapt down a spiral staircase. Black-Star caught up and flew down the staircase's central column, using Tsubaki's scythes to slow his descent. Spirit used his arm-blade to drop down.

At the bottom of the staircase, the squad could see a wide room, illuminated by an electric chandelier. At the opposite end was a yellow vault door, composed of gears and intricate machinery. In front of it stood a woman in a backless dress, showing off an ornate scorpion tattoo. Her braid glimmered in varying shades of magenta as it flicked back and forth about her head. She turned and glared at the squad that surrounded her. Her irises, cyan in the middle and blood red at the edges, emanated the pungent stench of pure crazy.

"Twenty minutes! Terrible work for DWMA's best," she intoned. Her smile widened as she locked gazes with Kiddo. "Back in my time, your father ran a far tighter ship. Maybe the old man has grown lax after ten millennia."

Black-Star frowned as he eyed Kiddo.

"Oi, who's the broad?" he asked.

"Someone who should be dead," said Kiddo. He stepped forward, trying his best not to tremble as he mumbled, "Shaula Gorgon, I presume?"

The woman gave a curtsey. "With pride, Death The Kid!"

"My father was certain he'd erased you and your sisters from this planet like the pee-stains you were," spat Kiddo.

Shaula grit her teeth and sneered. "True, he had taken my beloved sisters! The thought infuriates me more than sand in my vajayjay!" Her braid stood erect over her head like a scorpion tail. "Perhaps vengeance is in order? He takes my sisters, I take his son!"

The Witch suddenly vanished in a crash and a flood of smoke. Then Black-Star flew through the air toward the cloud, and brought his foot down upon Shaula's head.

"Damned if you ignore your God, mutha-trucka!" he roared. Tsubaki recovered from her flashbomb mode and retook sword form in Black-Star's hand. He swiped and slashed at the Witch, who dodged his blows with ease. Lucky for him, he was just as quick-witted, and dodged the jabs she made with her braid. Spirit went into the fray with his arm-blade. Shaula couldn't defend against both. Black-Star saw his opening and landed a decent hit to her stomach. Shaula flew toward the wall.

"Watch out!" shrieked Kiddo.

It was too late. Shaula's braid lashed out and penetrated

the calf of a nearby meister. She then deftly knocked him on his back before jabbing the two next to him. Kiddo fired relentlessly at her, but she kept using the meisters and weapons as human shields while jabbing them. The rest of the squad dove in to fight her, deaf to Kiddo's commands to stay back. The squad soon found themselves fighting against their own comrades, who blindly threw themselves in front of Shaula.

Kiddo struggled to get a clear shot amid the chaos. Even when he could clearly see Shaula approaching the vault door, an infected meister always managed to intercept the bullet. Shaula grinned as she pressed her hand to the vault door and proclaimed, "*Akoghalrab!*[5]"

With a shudder, the door broke into a pile of twisted metal and stripped gears. The infected meisters formed a barricade around the door as Shaula waltzed into the chamber beyond. Black-Star watched the intruder saunter into the DWMA vault, and grit his teeth with fury.

"Tsubaki, we gotta get them out of the way!" he yelled. "Chain-scythe form! We'll get this time right!"

"Got it!" replied Tsubaki and she transformed.

They matched their breathing and heart rates, and proclaimed, "Soul Resonance!"

Tsubaki's form glowed with a blue and yellow flame as her chain snaked its way through the rabble. It wove around the ankles of the infected meisters before charging back through the crowd toward Black-Star's waiting hand. Then he yanked the chain hard, knocking the infected off their feet. He hoisted them into the air, glared at Kiddo, Spirit, and the remaining squad, and roared, "Go!"

Kiddo led the charge into the vault. They followed the footprints in the dust through the shelves of treasures and heirlooms of DWMA, until they found the intruder. In her slender hands, she held an ornate hinged box sculpted from bronze. She caressed the edge of the box, and

---

[5]    See Appendix A on Witchese Language.

grinned with excitement.

"And it only took three millennia," she intoned.

Kiddo raised his guns. "Put the box back, now!"

"Or what?" intoned Shaula. She suddenly jerked her head to the side. In the antechamber, every single meister and weapon held in Tsubaki's thrall suddenly fell limp. Tsubaki's chain released them as she shrieked with panic. She retook her human form and tried to rouse them. Black-Star saw their heads and growled, "Their necks snapped."

Kiddo and Spirit's jaws dropped in horror.

"There's an eleven year old Demon Weapon in your bazaar, wreaking havoc," said Shaula. "I snap my fingers and her parents'll need a four-foot coffin."

Liz and Patty shuddered with horror, making it difficult for their mortified meister to hold them. He kept their barrels fixed on the Witch. Spirit and the remaining meisters kept their guard.

"I can't let you leave with that chest," stammered Kiddo.

"And I ain't gonna let you kill someone's daughter," growled Spirit.

Black-Star marched into the room, Tsubaki's sword form trembling in his hand. "And we ain't gonna let ya leave alive," said the ninja and his sword.

Shaula pursed her lips with frustration. Her eyes darted down to her watch, then looked back at Kiddo.

"*Ez agda solokt?*" she murmured under her breath.

Kiddo's ears perked up and he intoned, "Expecting someone?" Shaula looked surprised. "Oh yeah, I can understand Witchese," said Kiddo. "*Us ubpraz akzlidrig gtu raz ubbol dzikhatezo!*"

Shaula's smile widened, until she started to giggle. No one got a chance to ask why, before the shadows in the room came to life and pounced upon them. Black-Star and Tsubaki moved much faster, and managed to deflect most of the dark blades that charged toward them. Black-Star looked at Kiddo and yelled, "It's Masamune!"

From the corridor emerged an elderly woman, a black Japanese broadsword in her hands. The tattoos of Masamune flickered like flames along her wrinkled cheeks.

"Seriously, Masamune," moaned Shaula. "It took less time for me to pinch a loaf after two servings of haloumi!"

"This woman moves slowly," said the old woman in a deep monotone. The shadows beneath the squad suddenly writhed and sent them all through the air. They landed in a heap, but Masamune's shadowy knives came at them just as they regained their footing. Meanwhile, Shaula sauntered her way to Masamune's side, her loot in hand.

"Stop her!" screamed Kiddo. "She mustn't have that box!"

A furious rage built within Black-Star, and he launched off his feet toward Masamune. His soul wavelength blew out of control as he deflected the shadowy blades. He let out a tremendous roar that drowned out Tsubaki's desperate protests, and brought the blade of her sword form down on the old woman's head. With lightning speed, the lady parried the blow. The black sword crackled with dark lightning bolts that rippled along Tsubaki's form, and pervaded their resonance link.

Black-Star saw a little girl in a faint yellow kimono, collecting camellia flowers. When she offered the flowers to the blue-clad boy on the landing, she gave him a smile that seemed more desperate than honest.

"Immortal," said the boy warmly.

Reality came crashing back down on the pair. Black-Star hit the floor first. Tsubaki came down after, and hit him with a dull thud. A shower of glass shards rained from the cabinets either side of them, shattered from the force of Masamune's blast.

Shaula gazed at the chaos before her, and gave an amused chuckle. She looked to the old woman, who handed over the black sword.

"Keep them at bay a little longer, will you?" she said

before racing back down the corridor.

Kiddo and Spirit leapt to their feet and raced after the Witch. The old lady held up her hand, and her shadow morphed into a black wall that pushed them back. They tried to go around, but it just blocked any path they tried. Spirit roared and began hacking at it with his arm-blade, while Kiddo fired furiously into it. Be it the dwindling power of Masamune's influence or the force of their attack, the shadow shield soon disintegrated. All that was left behind was a very confused old lady.

"She can't have gone far!" said Spirit as he sprinted down the hall.

Kiddo glanced over at Black-Star. He had a confused look in his eyes as he gazed at his weapon, who sat beside him, clutching her chest as if she'd been heinously violated. Kiddo grit his teeth at the sight.

"Let's go, Kiddo," said Liz. "They won't be help any more."

With a sigh, Kiddo turned and raced down the hall. He caught up with Spirit, who tracked the Witch's footprints out of the catacombs, back to the central atrium, and out the westward passages. But by the time they reached the ventilation outlet, Shaula's trail was already gone.

\* \* \*

Exhausted, Maka fell to her knees. She struggled to hold onto Soul's scythe-form as Abhilasha came around for another attack. Maka parried the blows and swivelled to knock the girl off her feet. But her form was clumsy and tired, completely drained by the desire to not harm her student.

"For God's sake, Maka, just fight her!" snapped Soul.

"We can't hurt her," cried Maka.

The girl took advantage of the opening, kicked Maka's legs out from under her, and brought her blade down upon her. In a flash, Soul retook human form, save for his arm, with which he parried the blow. With a roar, he threw

Abhilasha through the air.

"Get the Hell away from my meister, bitch!" he snarled.

Abhilasha leapt to her feet and charged Soul. The albino raised his blade, ready for the attack. Abhilasha halted. She stepped away from Maka and Soul. She was silent a moment. Then her blade suddenly bisected her neck.

The group of girls nearby fell into a horrified frenzy as their friend fell to the ground. Maka scrambled over and tried to cover the girl's wounds with her hands. Soul grabbed his phone and called for an ambulance.

The crowd of bystanders just stood, immobile and flabbergasted, horrified by the carnage they'd witnessed.

## 10 | Drowning Sorrows

The Reaper shook his head with dismay. To his left, Maka stood hugging herself, pale faced with grief. Soul paced around nearby, stealing the odd glance at his meister and fuming with powerlessness. Black-Star stood silently, his eyes fixated on Tsubaki, who refused to make eye contact with anyone.

*Hmm … teenage drama has always been annoying,* thought the Reaper. *Though, not nearly as bad as Gilgamesh and Enkidu … Oh boy, weren't they grating!*

Kiddo and his weapons entered the Reaper's chamber, his eyes bloodshot from sleepless days and hair glossy with the accompanying lack of hygiene. Liz and Patty's cocky demeanour had been turned right down to zero.

The Reaper's son looked to Maka and intoned, "I'm sorry for the loss of your students."

Maka didn't reply. Even if she'd wanted to, she wouldn't have had the chance. Black-Star swooped in and socked Kiddo across the cheek.

"Forget 'sorries,' you asshole," he yelled as Liz pushed him off her meister's prone form. "What the Hell was that girl, and what did she kill a bunch of people for?"

"Would you like me to tell you, or should I offer you another cheek to punch?" snorted Kiddo as he sniffed back some blood.

Soul stepped forward and managed to calm the enraged

Black-Star. Patty pulled Kiddo up so he could straighten
out his symmetric attire, and he addressed the group.

"The woman who attacked DWMA today is Shaula
Gorgon," he began. "She is the youngest of the three
Gorgon Sisters, a trio of rogue Witches who terrorised the
ancient world. Shifting the planet's axis, blocking rivers,
the Bronze Age collapse. That was all them."

The Reaper chimed in, "The Original Eight and I took
them out finally. But ooh-eeh, was it hard! We beat the
elder two, for sure, but we never found the younger one's
body. Plus, we didn't get it done in time to stop those
rascals from starting a war between us and the Witches."

"Oh, yeah? So none of ya figured, 'hey, let's find this
third hag 'n' kill her'?" growled Black-Star. "Nah, that's
alright. We'll sit with our thumbs up our butts until she
murders a couple of people."

"Black-Star, be quiet," said the Reaper in a deep tone,
which sent chills down everyone's spines. The ninja fell
silent.

"How she evaded capture, we don't know," said
Kiddo. "But that doesn't matter now. She is the
brainwasher. Her braid appears to be a stinger that allows
her to infect others with a mind control agent."

Tsubaki cleared her throat and whispered, "What did
she steal?"

"A Demon Tool that, quite frankly, should have been
destroyed," replied Kiddo, his yellow orbs fixed on his
father. "The box she took contains the Shining
Trapezohedron of Eibon."

"The dimensional sorcerer, Eibon," murmured Maka in
a monotone.

"Ol' coot just loved messin' with space-time," said the
Reaper. "I remember that one was his first experiment
with pocket dimensions."

Soul scratched his head and moaned, "Yeah, I didn't
really follow that in class."

"The Trapezohedron is a space-time warping device,"

said Kiddo. "A primitive one, in that it could only create a pocket dimension, and only maintain it as long as the pathway between here and there remained closed." He noticed everyone's glazed eyes and huffed. "Think of it like a party balloon. You blow it up and tie it at the end. After that, the only way to enter the balloon is to pop it."

Soul palmed his fist. "Oh, now I get it."

"What would she want with that?" asked Patty. "She didn't seem like she was gonna throw a party."

"Maybe she plans to seal DWMA inside a pocket dimension," said Liz.

"Prob'ly not," said the Reaper. "That ol' Trap's already running a pocket dimension. And we'd best hope Shaula doesn't know how to pop the balloon."

Everyone gave confused glances, except for Kiddo, who explained, "The Trapezohedron, while a primitive warping device, is a perfect one-man prison. And it's currently holding Nyarlathotep."

Tsubaki, Black-Star, and Soul looked at Maka, whom they expected to have the answer. The normally perky girl gave a silent shrug and motioned for Kiddo to continue.

"Nyarlathotep is a monster of madness," said Kiddo. "Different from an Asura, but still quite dangerous. It spewed madness into the world and drove Neanderthals to extinction before Father and Eibon sealed it away."

Black-Star punched his palm and growled, "And since that Shaula just loves terrorising people, I'm sure she'd love to let that thing out."

"How would she release it?" asked Maka.

"She'd need a bunch of souls, all of them resonating at once, and sacrifice them all in one go," said the Reaper. "Just hope she ain't got enough."

Kiddo glanced at the Reaper. "I've put our remaining defences on high alert and issued a description of Shaula to the citizenry. We'll find her before she can activate the device." He, Liz, and Patty turned to leave.

"Oi, what should we be doing?" yelled Soul.

Kiddo looked over his shoulder and said, "Go home and get some rest. You all need to be ready."

* * *

Death City was *deathly* silent. American flags flew at half-mast on almost every porch lining the main street leading up to DWMA, where a shrine had been raised to Abhilasha and her victim, Tamika. Further out, Soul could see the DCPD working with the Reaper's teams to search for Shaula. His head felt sore with the image of that girl's blade through her own throat, and frustration that he couldn't find anything to say to his meister. She just sat there on the empty tram, wringing her hands and fidgeting.

He finally found the guts to say, "Maka, don't worry. We'll get the hag that did this."

Maka said nothing.

Soul went on, "And when we're done, I'll make you that pizza you really like: skittles, kale, and aioli!"

"Be quiet," Maka whispered, though it came across as a deafening roar.

She leapt off the tram as it reached their street, and she power-walked down the road toward their flat. Soul struggled to keep up with her, and every effort he made to comfort her earned him a cold shoulder. He started to get angry, his face heating up, when Maka almost slammed their apartment door shut on him. He glared at the blonde girl, who undid her pigtails and slumped over the kitchen countertop. He could hardly be bothered with her furious panting, and yelled, "Oi! I know it was bad you lost a student, but there's no need to be a bitch about it."

"Bitch?" intoned Maka as she turned to reveal her blood-red eyes and flushed cheeks. "Two little girls were murdered because we didn't catch that Witch soon enough. If we had stayed in the Reaper's chambers that night, and kept an eye on that kid, we could have stopped Shaula from finding her way in. Abhilasha and Tamika had their whole lives ahead of them, so excuse this bitch for grieving."

Soul's face softened and his body tingled with regret. He cleared his throat and said, "Look, I'm sorry. And I'm shaken too. But nothing I do can change it. What matters is getting this mission done."

"Yeah, you're really shaken," snapped Maka. "As shaken as if it'd been a boy?" Soul frowned as his lips downturned with disgust. Maka didn't give him a chance to retort. "Was just a bunch of girls that died, right? And *you* were the one yelling me to 'Fight! Fight! Fight!' How like a Goddamn man! All that matters is you the mission! You get your souls and become a Death Scythe! Forget the girls, they're dead! Hell, why even wait until they're dead before moving on? You don't even wait for the coroner's report. Screw that! You don't even wait until the last round of chemo's finished!"

The walls of their apartment reverberated with the sound of Maka's yells. They left a ring in Soul's ears overshadowed only by the confusion and indignation that ripped through his mind. All he could do was stare, slack-jawed, at the blonde whose cheeks were saturated with tears. Confusion gave way to anger, and he growled, "Go screw yourself, Albarn!" Then he swivelled and slammed the door shut behind him.

He didn't stay long enough to hear Maka's stifled sobs through the door.

\* \* \*

The classroom lights were off, yet the room was well illuminated by the orange light of the vigil just outside. The flickers of hundreds of candles projected an otherworldly dance of shadows on the walls. Aside from the sounds of hymns, prayers, and sobs of the crowd, the room was silent.

Tsubaki smirked at the relief she felt in that isolated space.

A monstrous thunderclap ripped through her serenity.

She looked at the door, which had been ripped off its hinges by Black-Star.

The ninja raised a clenched fist and bellowed, "Tsubaki! Your God hath descended-eth to soothe-eth your-est distresses … eth!"

A torrent of outraged expletives hit hard against Tsubaki's internal censor. It miraculously held as she sighed. She meekly held up her palm to signal her desire to be alone, which Black-Star ignored as he stomped up the stairs of the lecture theatre to her seat.

"My ninja senses have detected your distress!" he proclaimed. "Yet, your God is confused as to why being called 'Immortal' would cause you pain! Please enlighten me so that I may de-distress you!"

Tsubaki's breathing quickened as she kept her hands above her head.

"Please, Black-Star, I'm not in the mood," she whispered.

"I guess it must have been about that boy in your back-yard," said Black-Star, his boisterousness unwavering. Tsubaki's blood pressure spiked as he yelled, "I saw you gettin' him flowers. I'd bet it was Masamune who killed a guy you really liked, eh? That must be it!"

"No, it wasn't," Tsubaki moaned.

Black-Star grabbed her by the shoulders and shook her excitedly. "Then tell me! Speak to me! I know what to do! Just tell me what I can do!"

Tsubaki prised his hands away from her and pushed him savagely. He tumbled backwards over the chairs, and landed with his neck in an awkward position. Tsubaki was certain she heard a crack, and shrieked with worry. She leapt over the chairs with a cry, "Black-Star, are you alright?"

"Pah! A hurt neck'll never kill a God!" roared Black-Star as he jumped onto one of the chairs. A frazzled mess of emotions, Tsubaki started rubbing her temples as her tired brain searched for a way to shoo her meister off.

"Black-Star, you need to calm down," she said, though her voice was drowned out by the boy's incessant bellows and chortling.

His fists on his hips, he bellowed, "Curse that freakin' Masamune! That mutha-trucka hurt my weapon by callin' her 'Immortal!'"

Tsubaki snapped.

She grabbed the shorter boy by the scruff of his neck and threw him through the air. He landed head first on the teacher's desk, leaving a good clean imprint of his face in its wood. Black-Star shot up, blood freefalling out his nose, and yelled, "What the mutha-truckin' heck, Tsubaki? You coulda killed me!"

"It's called motherfucker!" screamed the girl. "It's motherfucker, you brain-dead, incompetent show-off! Every time you say it, it's like nails on a fucking chalkboard!"

Black-Star shut up.

"And, even though it's none of your Goddamn business, _Bang-Lee,_" Tsubaki bellowed, "Masamune didn't call me 'Immortal.' He called me 'Imouto[6].' It means 'Little Sister' in Japanese, you stupid jackass! Masamune is my older brother, who you saw in my memories. And if you want someone to curse, then frigging-well curse me. I was the one who inherited the Multiform ability of the Nakatsukasa Clan, not him. That's why he's hurting everyone! Those girls died because I just had to inherit this ability over him! And nothing, not me, not you, can change that!"

Black-Star forgot to breathe and almost passed out. As he struggled to catch his breath, he stammered, "But your God'll fix it. I'll make it better. We just have to get in gear."

Adrenaline flooded through Tsubaki's system, and without realising it, she ripped a chair out of the floor and

---

[6]  When using Japanese pronunciation, 'imouto' sounds very similar to 'immortal.'

threw it at him. He narrowly dodged it, stumbling off the desk and tumbling along the floor. He scrambled to his feet and saw Tsubaki coming at him.

"Get out!" barked the girl. "I don't want to deal with your crap anymore!"

"Tsubaki," Black-Star squeaked.

The girl's long braid suddenly turned into a chain-scythe that whipped around her head as she screeched, "Get away from me!"

The scythe blade only narrowly missed Black-Star's head. In the next instant, he was out the door, sprinting down the corridor in a panic. Tsubaki saw her chain-scythe blade embedded in the side of the desk. She willed it to become her hair once more as her anger vanished. She fell to her knees and cried.

"What have I done?" she sobbed.

* * *

Soul trudged into a bar about six blocks downtown of his apartment. A bright neon sign above the entrance read, 'The Creaking Coffin.' It even had an animated coffin, with a hand sticking out of it. Although he was underage, they still let him in, the bartender greeting him with a bittersweet smile.

"Open late?" he mumbled, some adrenaline remaining from his fight with Maka.

The bartender looked around his establishment with a smirk. The place had a few people grieving for the lost girls in their own way.

"On a night like this, I might as well be," he mumbled. "Though, I doubt my customers're here to listen to you play."

Soul eyed the piano and acoustic guitar on the small stage nearby. Memories of playing in front of a full house elicited a small smile. He took a seat at the bar and grumbled, "The usual."

The bartender handed Soul a can of Mountain Dew.

The boy downed it in seven seconds flat. The bartender let out an amused chuckle as he handed him another can.

"Too bad you can't drown your sorrows the old fashioned way," he said. "Some fellas, when hearin' about dead kids, ten jiggers of scotch ain't got nothin' on 'em."

Soul grit his sharp teeth and considered taking a bite out of his empty can. It'd probably have cut his mouth something awful, but he'd welcome the distraction. He looked up at the bartender and said, "Maka's taking it worse. The brainwashed kid was one of her students, and she couldn't fight her."

The bartender gasped, "You two saw it happen?"

"And looks like we're breaking up over it," Soul intoned, his voice cracking with mounting grief. At that, the bartender put two glasses between them, a large chunk of ice in each of them, and filled them with Jack-Daniels.

"Screw the law," he growled as he held up one of the glasses.

Soul shook his head, took the glass, clinked it to the bartender's, and upended it. The liquid was foul, and stung like needles screeching down his throat. He muscled it back, and panted fervently. Then, he looked at the bartender, and motioned for another glass.

After a third glass, Soul noticed Black-Star plonk down on the stool next to him. His face was blank with a look of defeat Soul never thought he'd see. The ninja mumbled, "You too?"

"Maka kicked me out," said Soul. "Said, I didn't care about girls. I'm like all men. Of course, I care about those girls. And I care about her too. What is she on? Jesus, that girl is one mega-crazy psycho-bitch." He downed another glass of scotch. Soul didn't notice the bartender take the bottle away as he continued to rant. "I don't even wait for the autopsy. She even yelled something about chemo. What the Hell is that? Seriously, the shit I put up with for her." He grabbed onto the bar to steady himself through a dizzy spell. He held back his sick and said, "Tsubaki lose her shit too, eh?"

Black-Star nodded.

"I'd never heard my Tsubaki swear before," he droned. "She doesn't realise I say 'mutha-trucka' so I don't offend her. She said it annoyed her. And she said it was her fault for Masamune goin' evil because she's his little sister."

"Jesus, seriously?" exclaimed Soul.

"She got the Multiform instead of him," said Black-Star. "And he got pissed and went evil. She thinks it's her fault."

Soul's eyes widened incredulously. "That's crap! She ain't got no control over her weapon form. She's just born with it. That don't make it her fault. And it's not her fault that those kids died."

"I wanted to tell her that and make her feel better, but she kicked me out," replied Black-Star. The words 'blame' and 'fault' echoed in his mind. Before he realised it, fury had gripped his body and his hands clenched. "You know what?" he growled. "It's not my fault either. Not yours. And it ain't Maka's." He thrust his finger in Soul's drunk face. "You know whose fault it is? That bastard, Death The Kid. If he hadn't sniped us –"

"We could've caught up our soul count," interjected Soul. "He wouldn't've dragged us into this stupid team."

"We wouldn't've found that kid at the docks and brought him in," yelled Black-Star. "Shaula wouldn't've gotten that guard."

"Wouldn't've stolen that thing from DWMA," growled Soul. "Those kids wouldn't've died."

Black-Star punched his fist and his muscles flexed with rage. Soul's hand turned into a scythe-blade that glimmered in the dim light of the tavern. Their eyes locked resolutely.

"Let's finish what we started," growled Black-Star.

In an instant, they were out the door. Silently, the bartender put two soft drinks and three scotches on Soul's tab.

# 11 | Seven Per Cent

At one in the morning, the corridors of DWMA would normally have been empty. But the ongoing search for Shaula had spurred the Reaper to keep round-the-clock security. That, and the vigil continued for the two dead girls.

Soul and Black-Star hardly noticed the ongoing hymns and grieving as they barged past the security checkpoints. They navigated the corridors of the castle until they found a relatively empty walkway. Only two meister and weapon pairs were posted at each end of the corridor. At the exact mid-point of the hallway was a single door, the sign above it reading, 'Office of Death The Kid.'

With a growl, Black-Star sprinted down the corridor, Soul close behind. They stopped when they almost tripped over Liz's leg. The girl woke with a start and rubbed her very tired eyes. She looked up and saw the furious boys.

"Hmph, you here for a go?" she yawned. She checked her sister. Patty was still out-cold, a long flow of drool starting at her mouth and going all the way down Liz's shoulder. She rolled her eyes and turned to the boys. "Kiddo's in his office, but don't expect us to get involved."

"He won't be a match for God, then," snapped Black-Star.

"Yeah, 'cause he ain't got no hoes to hide behind," spat

Soul.

Liz shot them the middle finger, a bored look on her face, before she snuggled up to Patty and went back to sleep.

Soul and Black-Star barged through the office doors and roared, "Your day of reckonin' is here, Kiddo!"

They saw something that, in hindsight, they should have expected. But it surprised them so much that their fighting spirits left them, like air from a burst balloon.

Kiddo's jacket and shirt lay beside the door, crumpled and decrepit. The man himself stood in his pants and sweatshirt, both of which were stained yellow. His body trembled as if he were seizing as he tried to operate a laser surveyor, which was focused on his desk. His breathing was shaky, punctuated by the occasional groan when he shifted the delicate knobs a little too far. He looked out from behind the surveyor, his normally pale complexion an utter mess of wrinkles and lines.

He stomped over to his desk and touched its side very slightly. He tapped it a little more, before giving it a solid push. The furniture moved only a slight amount. Then the Reaper's son charged back to the surveyor and looked through its eyepiece, only to blurt an expletive.

Soul swallowed heavily at the sight, and coughed up the courage to ask, "Ah, Kiddo, can we talk a sec?"

Kiddo's glare darted their way, and he panted fervently. "It really isn't a good time."

"No! We got a bone to pick with you!" blurted Black-Star, but his will was far less than it had been thirty seconds ago. He couldn't take his eyes off the surveyor, and couldn't help but ask, "The Hell's with this?"

Kiddo scrambled to the desk and pushed it slightly in the opposite direction. He braced against the desk for a bit of support, caught his breath, and then walked back to the surveyor.

"Oh, come on," he cried when he looked into the device again. He stepped away and leaned on his knees, sweat freefalling from his brow. He looked at Soul and Black-Star, who were completely befuddled. "It's been a bad day, and it took hours to finish all the paper work. I'm tired, upset, and I just want to go home! But …" – he glared at the desk – "I can't get my desk right in the middle of the office."

Soul raised an eyebrow. "Looks okay to me, dude."

Kiddo looked back to the surveyor, and tried to turn some more knobs. His hands shook so much they rattled the device's frame. The device's tripod legs creaked slightly.

Suddenly, Kiddo let out a deafening scream. He grabbed one of the tripod legs and smashed the device into the ground. Then he bludgeoned the desk into oblivion. Then he pulverised his bookshelf. With a final shriek, he embedded the ruined surveyor in the drywall.

Black-Star huddled close to Soul, whose scythe-arm was at the ready. But neither could be sure what they were ready for. His hands on his knees, Kiddo cringed, panted, and groaned from what had to be serious internal pain. Tears mingled with sweat drops that trickled down his cheeks. He rubbed them away and forced himself to stand erect. He approached the pair slowly, but couldn't bring his eyes to meet theirs.

"Sorry," he mumbled. "Bad day, people dying, frigging asymmetry all around. Shaula didn't even have the decency to kill an equal number of men and women." His teeth almost shattered under the force of his clenched jaw. "God, I hate the number seven."

Soul couldn't find words, but the far-simpler Black-Star said, "Yeah, we get it, not symmetrical. Dude, you need help."

Kiddo glared at Black-Star and snarled, "Lots of digits aren't symmetrical, Black-Star. Hell, depending on the font you use, not even eight is. That's not why I hate seven."

"Then, why?" stammered Soul.

"Seven per cent," growled Kiddo. "*That* is the portion

of Asura Eggs that come from career criminals, sociopaths, rapists, and terrorists. Do you know where the rest come from? Rape victims, abused kids and spouses." The tears flowed faster. "Everyone goes on about May-Second, while I've handled about six Asura Eggs that came from Afganistan veterans! Do you have any idea how many times I wished I'd seen Osama Bin Laden's name on Father's list? At the very least, I wanted to see a schoolyard bully from a rich family!

"Asura Eggs happen because wretched people dump their own garbage on everyone else. These bastards traumatise and terrorise, and then get to go on and live happy lives. The victims try their best to carry on and end up going mad. And we hunt them down to stop the madness spreading, but this world is already mad."

Kiddo bit his lip to fight his tears back, while his entire body ticked and shuddered. He looked at the two dumbstruck boys and said, "This world *is* unfair. I'm mature enough to realise that, otherwise I'd be spending all my time complaining online about it. But I also try my best not to dump my issues on everyone else. And I *know* I don't do a good job of it. But I try."

With that, he swivelled and walked toward a box in the corner. He opened it to reveal another set of surveying equipment. Black-Star and Soul choked at the sight of him setting it up to continue his desk alignment procedure. Seeming not to notice his pulverised desk, he let out a long sigh of exhaustion and said, "So, what did you two need to talk about again?"

Soul's chest ached with horror at the sight. He stepped forward and stammered, "Kiddo."

Black-Star put a hand on his shoulder and stopped him.

"We got nothin', Kiddo," said the ninja softly. "Sorry we disturbed ya."

"Yeah, see ya tomorrow," stammered Soul.

The pair left, closing the door behind them, and began trudging down the hall. Soul saw Liz out the corner of his eye, a soft smile on her face.

"Uh, Liz," he mumbled. "Look ... Sorry about calling you a hoe. I was mad, and it wasn't right."

Liz's tired smile widened and she waved him off.

"Don't worry about it," she chuckled. "Thinking about some of the things I've been called, 'hoe' is kind of like a complement." She gazed at the door and sighed. "Patty and I were, like, the best muggers this side of Brooklyn. Lost count of the number of times the mob tried to get us, but we ... you know ... *obviously* beat them back. Then, one day, we pissed off the wrong don, and ... let's just say the price on our heads would've made Gordon Gekko shit himself. But Kiddo, he appeared, and took out all the gangsters they sent after us. He let us stay at his place, which we did. But I was only there to steal what we could and take off. You know what? He caught us stealing shit, and offered us more!" She chuckled incredulously, though tears neared her eyes. "He actually sat there while we're taking his stuff, and hands us a freaking blank cheque!"

Black-Star's jaw dropped while Soul remained silent.

Liz went on, "Mom abandoned us at a slum; punks looking for bitches to slap and bang; assholes taking advantage of us ... and there's this kid who should've called the cops but didn't. All he was asking was to be his partners, and probably do some good."

Liz came back to the present, and saw the looks on the boys' faces. She chuckled gauchely. "Yeah, here I am, unloading." She gazed at the door once again. "He's the best thing that ever happened to us. We've met all these great people in Death City, thanks to him. We ain't needed to steal or cheat anyone since. He's done that much. I guess, dealing with his crazy OCD crap is worth it."

Soul smiled. He held out his hand, and said, "You know, we never actually introduced ourselves. Soul Evans is my name."

Liz shook his hand. "Elizabeth Thompson. This sleepyhead is my sister, Patricia."

Black-Star offered his next and said, "Bang-Lee Wong. Nice to meet you."

The boys stepped back and bade the girl good night. They left the DWMA building in silence, speaking only to say "See you tomorrow" before parting. Soul reached his apartment.

There was Maka, snuggled up on the couch, Blaire in cat form nestled against her stomach. Soul stood there a while, staring at the girl and the dried tear streaks that marred her face. He took a blanket from their shared linen cupboard and gently draped it over her, before retreating to his room and passing out on his bed.

## 12 | Witch Hunt

Soul rose late the next morning to the smell of scrambled eggs. He trudged out of his bedroom and into the kitchen, finding Maka silently chomping at her breakfast. None had been left out for him.

"You didn't make any for me?" he mumbled.

"Make it yourself," snapped the blonde. "I'm too busy being a *bitch*."

Nearby, Blaire let out a sound partway between a sigh and a purr. Soul let it go, however, because he knew he deserved a bit of a cold shoulder. He fixed himself a bowl of corn flakes, and sat at the table beside his meister. She wouldn't even glance his way, and made an obvious show of pretending he wasn't there. He told himself she was just angry, and she'd get over it if she had her space. Another part of his mind yelled at him to discuss Shaula at the very least.

"No update on Shaula yet?" he stammered.

"There's no imprint of a book on your lazy head, so obviously not," snarled Maka.

She stood up to bus her plate, but Soul grabbed her hand and gripped it tightly so that she couldn't pull away. He noted her subtle trembling, and knew she was stifling the urge to beat him up. He steeled his resolve and locked his eyes on her.

"We'll get that Witch," he said. "Together, we'll cut her

head off."

Then he released her arm. She slowly pulled away and made a beeline for her bedroom. He kept his gaze on her bedroom door a while longer, before returning to his breakfast.

"You know, she fell asleep waiting for you last night," said Blaire as she scratched her twitching ears.

"I know," mumbled Soul. He smiled at the magic cat. "Thanks for looking after her." The usually flirtatious creature just returned the smile before scooting across the living room and out onto the balcony. She darted onto the railing and descended the drainpipes outside, no doubt off to score some fish from the lonely widower at the seafood shop.

Soul showered quickly, threw on a clean shirt, jeans, and his black and yellow jacket. He emerged from his room to see Maka, her black long coat over her checkerboard skirt, blouse and tie combo. Her look was pensive despite being dressed in her war clothes. She eyed him nervously, before opening the door.

"We should get going," she mumbled. She exited the apartment, Soul locking the door behind them.

They said nothing on the tram up to DWMA. The silence was made worse by the emptiness of the carriage, since everyone else was still mourning. Soul stole an occasional glance Maka's way, but saw only the back of her head. The tram's brakes ground with a deafening squeal out the front of the Reaper's fortress, where a battalion of meisters and weapons, thirsty for Witch blood, laid in wait for an inevitable attack.

Inside the atrium of the castle, Kiddo stood as a military general presiding over his troops. His clothes were clean, his face was free of wrinkles, and his eyes radiated a determined gaze. It was as if the broken man from last night was just a doppelganger for the real Death The Kid.

"Hey," said Maka, breaking Soul out of his daze. Her voice was stern, but her face had a softer expression. "I'll report to Kiddo. You find Black-Star and Tsubaki." And she trotted off with a slight hint of the characteristic spring to her step.

Soul smiled as his red orbs scanned the atrium for their friends. Those friends appeared behind him. Tsubaki had a wide smile, though the muscles in her face looked too tired. The liveliness of her voice seemed dialled up to eleven as she chirped, "Good morning, Soul!"

She must have sucked all the energy out of Black-Star, who was unusually lax. His lips were pursed as if he were silencing himself. Tsubaki let off a few platitudes meant to motivate, before sprinting off in Maka's direction. Black-Star cringed at the sight, and mumbled, "Soul, am I a horrible guy?"

"Horrible ninja? Yes. Guy? Not a chance," said Soul. "She accept your apology?"

"I didn't even get a chance," moaned Black-Star. "As soon as I got home, I found her cooking dinner for me. She was all making like she was the piece of shit, dissing herself. I almost thought she was gonna kneel at my feet or something."

Soul rolled his eyes. "Well, that's what you get for calling yourself 'God,' dipshit."

Black-Star let out a frustrated sigh and kicked his feet against the ground. It did little to lift his gloomy mood, so he went outside and started to pace. Soul watched him go, and then glanced over at Maka and Tsubaki chatting. Behind them, Kiddo conversed with Liz and Patty.

*We've gotta get that Witch,* he thought. *But I don't know if Maka and I can synchronise with her in this mood.*

He kept thinking about their fight. It replayed in his head like a broken record. He mulled and mulled and mulled.

*Goddammit, Maka, could you make less sense? I get it. Your old man ain't a decent role model. So what freaking else is new? Didn't your Mom ever teach you not all men are douchebags?*

His breath caught in his throat. The fight replayed in

his head once more. Everything became a fuzzy, muffled blur of screaming and shouting. Then he reached the important part:

*You get your souls and become a Death Scythe! Forget the girls, they're dead! Hell, why even wait until they're dead before moving on? You don't even wait for the coroner's report. Screw that! You don't even wait until the last round of chemo's finished!*

Soul's eyes widened with realisation and he glanced over at Maka. There stood the blonde, her arms folded and her expression disgusted, as she glared at Spirit. The Reaper's personal weapon was giving her a pep talk she clearly hadn't asked for and didn't want. Then he hugged her – something that made Maka homicidal.

Soul sneered at the sight of Spirit Albarn.

*I get it, Maka,* he thought. *But I'll show you: it's not the form that matters, it's the soul.*

\* \* \*

A menacing crescent Moon ruled the night sky. Within a warehouse in the eastern outskirts of Death City, a group of cloaked figures knelt in a circle. They mumbled in deep tones as their eyes locked on the box in the centre, laid upon a placement of ornate red felt. It's carvings of cephalopods and menacing eyes glimmered in the light of a dozen candles set about it.

Shaula stood before the box, its very presence arousing her dark soul. She held up her hands and reached out through the aether to the twenty people around her. As malleable as putty, their poisoned souls responded to her will, and grew brighter in the void. The tendrils of her soul flicked and lashed against their obedient ectoplasms, cropping and grooming them as she would a forest of bonsai trees.

Her lips pursed with disappointment, and a dash of nervousness. A girl stood in the corner, whose face was marred by tattoos courtesy of the long Japanese sword in her hand. She noticed Shaula's dismay.

"You should not have sacrificed so many of your minions," said the girl with a deep masculine voice.

"Nitocris was supposed to be the source," retorted Shaula. She looked over her shoulder and sneered, "You could put in a little, Masamune."

Masamune's puppet raised a hand in refusal, before moving to the warehouse entrance. Over her shoulder, she said, "Take your time. I have sight where there are shadows. I will keep watch."

Shaula harrumphed and returned to tending her garden of souls. She tested the resonance link between her minions again. It had indeed grown. Yet, there were still outlying harmonics. They needed more focus.

Her ethereal senses prickled. One of her scorpion sentries chirped through her resonance link, and showed her an image of a street two blocks down. A group of DCPD officers sauntered down the road, checking each warehouse on the way to her stronghold.

Rather than panic, she licked her lips.

"Masamune," she chuckled. "Be a doll and bring me those police officers."

Masamune's puppet grinned. Through her scorpion friends, Shaula watched as the very shadows beneath the officers' feet lashed out and gagged them. The ghostly umbrae dragged the flailing cops down the street, into the warehouse, and presented them to Shaula. There were twelve in all. With a delightful squeak, the Witch jabbed each of them with her hair-stinger. When they succumbed to the venom, she snapped, "Join the resonance circle."

The new recruits formed another row of supplicants about the demonic box. An orgasmic chill raced up Shaula's spine as the link filled with more energy. But it was still not enough.

"Masamune, bring more," she said. The puppet left to prowl while Shaula glared at the growing ceremony.

*You have time,* she told herself. *You have watched this city fester for centuries, like a poo-stain on your panties that just won't wash off. Now, you're finally bringing the OxiClean. And you, who falsely calls himself 'Reaper,' sitting on a throne built on my sisters' graves, will finally go down the drain.*

* * *

The mood in the Reaper's chamber was tense. Maka sat on the floor, reaching out with her soul perception. But all that did was tell her that Shaula was somewhere on the outskirts of the city. Tsubaki fidgeted, while Black-Star meditated silently beside her. Kiddo stood motionless beside his father, listening for any and all updates from the advance scouts.

Soul stood to the side, the wheels in his head turning, his eyes fixed on his meister. He occasionally stole a glance in Liz and Patty's direction. They stood ready for their meister's call.

Kiddo suddenly looked up and gasped. He listened into his earpiece.

"Where?" he barked. After a brief pause, he exclaimed, "Shit!"

Everyone stood at attention.

"What up?" asked Black-Star.

"We've lost three scout units!" cried Kiddo. He cursed and growled. "She would have turned them, and then used them for her summoning ceremony. And *I* practically gift-wrapped them. Damn it!"

Before Liz and Patty could get close to their meister, Black-Star was already in motion. He placed his hand on Kiddo's shoulder and yelled, "Oi! Keep your cool!" Kiddo turned to retort, but couldn't displace the ninja's hand. Black-Star looked fixedly into Kiddo's yellow orbs and said, "We can still get her."

Maka chimed in, "Damn straight we can."

"How?" asked a very tired Kiddo.

"Those scouts were lost, where?" asked Maka. "Wherever they got lost —"

Kiddo excitedly thrust a finger in her face. "That's

where Shaula is! And they all went missing on corner of Methuselah and Teresias, East City."

Not needing a command from their meister, Liz and Patty assumed their gun forms in Kiddo's hands.

Black-Star raced over to Tsubaki and bellowed, "Let's get that big bro of yours!" With a shaky smile, the girl transformed into a chain-scythe.

Maka and Soul lingered a moment longer to watch the others race down the corridor. Soul stuck his hands in his pockets and gazed back at the Reaper, an aloof gleam in his eyes.

"Expect good things from us, Lord Reaper," he droned.

"We'll beat that Witch," said Maka confidently.

With a flash, Soul morphed into his scythe form, and Maka raced after the others. And yet, despite the matching resonance of their souls, Maka could not see the plot Soul was hiding deep within.

## 13 | Sibling Rivalry

Maka and Black-Star leapt off the vehicle just as the driver hit the breaks. Their momentum carried them into a sprint down Methuselah Street. Maka could now very clearly sense the slippery, decaying scent of Shaula's soul, along with over two dozen resonating spirits, in a warehouse halfway down the street.

They stopped dead in their tracks when they saw the ripples in the shadows. The Moon above was starting to set, sending those living umbrae teetering their way.

Kiddo swooped in on his hover board. From his vantage point, he could see the entire block. Into his earpiece, he grumbled, "Bring in the fog lights."

Within minutes, a fleet of helicopters sliced their way through the air. They came to hover over the block, and blasted a ray of photons down on the district of warehouses. The shadows seemed to shriek and growl as they scampered away from the burning light.

"All units, maintain a perimeter and keep an eye on your shadows," said Kiddo. Then, he dropped down to join Maka and Black-Star, in front of whom the lights cleared a long path down the street.

"Maka, Kiddo, you two take Shaula," said Black-Star. "Leave that mutha-trucka Masamune to me and Tsubaki."

"Got it!" grunted Maka.

Then they sprinted down the street.

The shadows stirred in the right of their field of vision. Kiddo spun in mid-air, his skateboard flying through the air and bisecting the shadowy tendrils that lashed toward them. He let off a volley of energy blasts to the others coming from behind, while Black-Star growled, "Tsubaki, Shuriken mode!"

Tsubaki morphed into a massive star-shaped blade that Black-Star threw forward. Tsubaki sliced through almost every black tentacle blocking their way, and Maka cleared up the rest with Soul's scythe blade. The forest of living darkness did little to hamper their advance toward the distinctive musk of Shaula's soul.

Tsubaki sensed the source of the shadows.

"Black-Star, up there," chirped her blade. Her meister looked up to the roof of the building to their right, and saw the silhouette of a child. She held a Japanese sword, twice as long as she was tall.

"Come to me, Imouto," she chuckled with a deep masculine tone.

Black-Star didn't even wait for Tsubaki to say she was ready, before he leapt onto a dumpster, bounced off it, and sprung into the air over the roof. The girl looked right at him. The fading moonlight reflected menacingly off the tattoos marring her cheeks. Deep red eyes glared at the ninja as he flew toward her. Black-Star flipped through the air, the sounds of his roars mingling with those of Tsubaki as he brought her chain-scythe blades down on the puppet.

With one hand, the puppet parried his blows. Nausea permeated Black-Star's body as black lightning crackled from the dark blade and coursed through his soul. The puppet flicked her wrist and launched him away.

"Jesus, what was that?" exclaimed Black-Star as he pulled himself to his feet. They shuddered with fatigue.

"That is the power of the Uncanny Blade," mumbled Tsubaki. Her face reflected in the blade of her chain-scythe form, and radiated a mournful expression. "That blade was once so beautiful. Now, it's reflection of his soul – black and decayed."

The puppet's head bobbled. Her grin widened like that of a poorly painted scarecrow.

"Tsubaki, how do we get it off her?" asked Black-Star.

"Masamune has latched his soul onto hers like a parasite," said Tsubaki. "But if you use your Big-Wave attack, you can break his hold. She'll drop the sword and he'll lose his power."

Black-Star chuckled excitedly and twirled Tsubaki's chain-scythes. "Then let's get this mutha-trucka!"

"Let's do it!" bellowed Tsubaki.

Masamune's puppet flew into motion. The tattoos on her face scrunched under the sheer force of her frown and grin as she brought the blade up toward Black-Star's abdomen. The ninja deftly blocked the blade with Tsubaki's chain and swiftly kicked the puppet's knees. The girl staggered as Black-Star flicked his wrist and swung the chain-scythe at her. She dodged just in time, flipped over, and then came at Black-Star a second time.

Tsubaki matched her wavelength with Black-Star's, their breathing in perfect synch as they fought. Yet, part of her mind wandered to a past filled with regret.

*This is why I came to DWMA,* she thought. *I had to hunt him down and stop him. This is my penance.*

"Tsubaki!" growled Black-Star, having sensed her thoughts through their resonance link. "You and me, we both know that's a load of crap!"

Black-Star swung the chain-scythe around, keeping the puppet at bay. Any attack Masamune mounted, Black-Star just swatted away and advanced further. The ninja came within arms reach, and summoned every ounce of his soul into his fist.

"Black-Star! Big wave!" he roared.

"Fool!" quipped Masamune.

A rain of shadowy spikes erupted from beneath the ninja and skewered him through the arms, thighs, and feet. Red fluid splashed across the iron roof. With a shriek,

Black-Star leapt away from the foe, who licked the shadows clean of his blood.

"Black-Star! Are you alright?" exclaimed Tsubaki.

"The Hell is this?" growled Black-Star. He was sure he was hallucinating, because he saw a spindly creature rise out of the darkness at the puppet's feet. It leered menacingly at him.

"Did you forget my power of shadows?" murmured Masamune.

The shadow beast lunged forward with tremendous speed. Black-Star had no choice but to dodge. But blood was oozing fast from his wounds. His head started to spin.

*No, Gods don't get dizzy!*

He slipped on a puddle of his blood and slid down the edge of the building. A chimney stopped his fall in the worst possible way for a man. Another, far worse pain ripped through his body from between his legs.

"Mega wedgie!" he shrieked.

"Black-Star, watch out!" cried Tsubaki.

The ninja parried the shadow's claws just in the nick of time. The beast pressed against him, and his strength dwindled while his fury grew.

*Come on! You're a God! Gods don't just do the impossible! They make a world for their followers!*

He twisted his wrists slightly, and the beast's claws flew into the metal beside his head. He spun onto his feet and landed on the chimney. Masamune's puppet flew through the air, ready to cleave his head in two.

"I'll make my new world!" he roared. "Tsubaki, now!"

They roared: "Soul Resonance!"

Yellow and blue light burst from Black-Star's eyes and merged with the chain-scythe. The chain grew to immense length and made a star-shaped shield between them and Masamune. The dark blade fizzled and sparked as it clattered against the barrier.

*Got ya now!*

With a delighted yawp, Black-Star released Tsubaki and

launched himself through the barrier. His entire being flew into his fists and he bellowed, "Big-Wave!"

His blow connected with the puppet's abdomen, and the girl squalled at the deep blue sparks that shocked her. With a black flash, the Uncanny Sword fell from her hands, right into Tsubaki's waiting grasp. Black-Star landed, the unconscious girl in his arms, and gasped at Tsubaki, holding the Uncanny Sword. She smiled at him as the black tattoos invaded her skin.

"Thanks, Black-Star," she said. "I'll take it from here."

Black-Star's jaw dropped in horror as his weapon partner screamed. A white flame enveloped and disintegrated her body, before plunging into the sword with a strident hiss. The sword clattered on the steel roof, inert.

Black-Star fell to his knees, mortified. He dropped the disoriented girl and hobbled toward the sword, fearing the worst. His hand edged toward the dark blade. The sensations it radiated nauseated him. And yet, he could feel, within the sinister resonance, the bright yellow soul of his weapon.

*So, that's what ya meant by penance,* he thought. He sat in front of the sword and glued his eyes to it. He did not move a muscle, and ignored the chaos that erupted around him: the tremors of the monster that stomped over buildings, the calls for all units to converge on Methuselah Street, even Kiddo's pleas for help.

"I ain't movin', Tsubaki, until you come back to me," he proclaimed.

* * *

A shallow sea of blood licked at Tsubaki's ankles. Around her stood a forest of withered trees. Not a single branch had a shade of green to complement the dead black wood. She gazed around. Cold, stagnant air filled her lungs and scratched at her skin. Her ears hummed with a low, strident ring.

"Welcome to my soul, my sister," grumbled a man seated on a brittle bough nearby. His arms emerged from beneath his white cloak, and a black Japanese sword materialised in his hand. His broadbrim hat fell from his head, revealing a gaunt face decorated by a tired sneer and black, lid-less eyes.

Tsubaki trembled sorrowfully. "It has been too long, Elder Brother." She held her hands out, and chain-scythes materialised. With a sigh, she proclaimed, "Uncanny Sword Masamune, you have conspired with a rogue Witch and engaged in evil activities. In the name of Lord Reaper, I claim your soul!"

She lunged forward, a cloud of bloody vapour wafting in her wake. His feet planted firmly, Masamune blocked the blows she brought. His expression changed little, even as Tsubaki threw all her strength into her attacks. He harrumphed with boredom, and swiped his sword once. Tsubaki flew backwards, a trail of blood flying from a deep gash to her belly.

Masamune sneered as the girl tried to pull herself to her feet.

"Did I teach you nothing?" he growled.

Tsubaki shuddered, and then attacked again with a shriek. Masamune deflected the blow and kneed her in the stomach. She flew again and landed headfirst in the bloody bog.

"Pitiful," murmured Masamune. "How many years at DWMA? And for what?"

Tsubaki's arms were out of strength. They buckled under her weight as she pushed up from the ground. Tears mingled with the red liquid marring her face.

"I joined DWMA to stop you," she cried. "It's *my* fault you turned out this way." She gripped her chain-scythes as tight as she could but they barely stayed in her hands. "*I* made you this way," she said. "I have to stop you."

In a blink, Masamune cleared the gap between them, and swiped and slashed savagely. Tsubaki's blood gushed from every puncture site and mingled with the watery, dilute red sea. She watched its colour slowly fade, and felt her soul vanish further and further into the dark void that her elder brother had become.

"Such arrogance," sneered Masamune. "It's always about you. *You* received the Multiform, while I was reduced to a mere Uncanny Sword. Yet I did my diligence as an elder brother, and attempted to school you." His breath faltered and he grit his teeth furiously. His blade drifted down to her cheek and slit it meticulously. "But you never listened," he snarled. "You never took anything to heart. You just made like a know-it-all and acted like you needed no one. My efforts wasted on an ungrateful whelp like you. You made me look like a fool."

Tsubaki's heart faltered as the tears flowed even more. Her memories played in reverse, skipping over everything except the darkest parts of her life: a mother's corpse; a father's belly slit by his own hand; a brother feasting on souls in fading Moonlight.

*It's my fault*, she thought. *I didn't try hard enough. I knew he only meant well, but he didn't need to teach me anything. I just wanted to follow my own path. If I hadn't been so prideful and just accepted what he said, my family would … That's why I picked Black-Star as my meister. That's why I picked Soul and Maka as my friends. They'd make me follow.*

Her mind fell on a fuzzy image of a boy, sitting on the back porch of a house in the countryside of Gunma. She plopped a camellia flower on his lap and smiled as hard as she could. The boy just sneered back at her.

*If I'd just done as I was told*, thought Tsubaki.

A cocky voice ripped through the void, as if belched from one who considered himself a rock-star.

"Ain't that a load of crap!" it yelled.

She turned and saw a boy in baggy white pants and a sleeveless black shirt that showed off his well-built physique. He picked a flower and beamed at it.

"Camellia flowers! That's 'tsubaki' in English, right?"

he asked her. He looked at the bush from where the flowers bloomed. "Ya know, pretty nice, ain't they? People're like, 'They ain't got no smell, so they're crap.' But why should they be the way everyone else wants? Why can't they do what they like? Follow their own path?"

Tsubaki pursed her lips. She couldn't keep eye contact with Black-Star. Behind her, she heard a voice that filled her with nostalgic dread. She turned and saw her mother, chiding a much younger version of herself. The voice was muffled, most of the words indistinguishable from noise. But she could hear certain phrases: *"Mind your brother! He's going to so much effort for you! He knows better about being a Demon Weapon!"*

"Obviously not," yawned Black-Star. "I mean, look where the shithead is now." He patted Tsubaki on the shoulder and murmured, "You should pick your own path."

Tsubaki moaned, "I wanted to. And I told him I would. I said I didn't need him or his help. That's why he … And I came to DWMA to train, so that I could stop him."

"Bullshit, you did," growled Black-Star. He glared into her eyes. "Remember the day we met? No one wanted to listen to my amazing performance of unholy Godliness. But you did. You didn't need to but you did. You had ten people asking you to be their weapon, but you came to me instead. You looked so happy when I asked you. Was that all just to get back at this mutha-trucka?"

An image of Black-Star, standing atop the skull of DWMA and proclaiming his Godhood, burst through Tsubaki's mind. She hadn't been able to stifle her chuckles at his blatant honesty. His brazenness and sheer ego felt like a breath of fresh air. He was so sure of himself, so confident that he could succeed; she just had to go along for the ride. She wanted to see if he really was a God.

Pleasant visions followed in quick succession: Black-Star's insane antics, day in and day out; Soul's music at *The Creaking Coffin*; Maka's half-decent attempt at Japanese fried noodles. She recalled laughter and smiles from her own lips – they felt miles apart from the forced smiles she offered a scowling Masamune.

She looked up at Black-Star from her place on the porch. But her meister no longer stood before her. Instead, she saw a mirror image of herself, wearing Black-Star's signature grin.

"Comin' to Lord Reaper's place for penance?" bellowed her doppelganger. "Total crap! Ya know why we came here?" The grin widened. "To live on our own mutha-truckin' terms."

The sea of blood suddenly exploded. A maelstrom of crystal-clear water flung the red outwards toward the infinite horizon. The dead trees disintegrated in the wake of Tsubaki's roar. Masamune flew backward, bewildered and overwhelmed.

Tsubaki stood over him, her ninja sword in hand. Her wounds sealed without a trace.

"I never asked for help," said Tsubaki. "All I ever wanted to do was be my own person. And maybe … yeah, it still is my fault you ended up this way. Maybe if I had just said so, you'd be fine now." She smiled solemnly. "I'm sorry, Elder Brother. But now, I am following my own path. Yours ends here."

Masamune roared and black sparks enveloped his body. He lunged forward, his blade targeting her heart. She deflected the blow and thrust her elbow into his chest. The recoil sent Masamune staggering backwards, and Tsubaki pressed her attack. She swatted his sword aside and brought her own across his face, then chest, and then stomach. She parried a frontal blow and head-butted him back.

Masamune's fury grew, and his eyes flashed purple. His body started to grow until it was twice as tall as Tsubaki.

"I will have your soul!" he screamed. His blade came down like a meteorite. Tsubaki launched herself upwards, past the ballistic sword, and with a mighty roar embedded her ninja sword in Masamune's chest.

The realm fell silent. The once red sea turned deep blue, save for the tiny patch of black where Masamune lay. His black eyes gazed up at his sister.

"So, your path is to follow someone else," he stammered. "Follow this boisterous attention-seeker? He doesn't need you, Tsubaki."

"No more than I needed you," said Tsubaki. "You needed me way more. But I could stand on my own. I did it so well I had enough time to be a chronic people pleaser." Her expression softened. "Maybe he doesn't need me … but he wants me. And I don't really need him, or *them* for that matter. But that's why I want them."

Masamune sighed. His body started to disintegrate in the water. And yet, he seemed almost intrigued. With his last breath, he said, "Seems like *tsubaki* flowers aren't as humdrum as I thought."

Then he was gone.

His sword remained, its blade shining vibrantly in the light of the sun above Tsubaki's head.

\* \* \*

Black-Star had long since lost track of time. It might have had something to do with the rather large lumps of rubble that had struck his head while he sat. Yet, even as blood gushed down his face, he did not move a muscle. His eyes remained fixed on the sword in front of him, disregarding everything around him – even the horrendous beast smashing the city behind him.

Suddenly, the sword gleamed. Then it flashed with bright yellow light, before assuming Tsubaki's form. She let out a long sigh.

"You're back!" exclaimed Black-Star.

Tsubaki smiled. "Yep, I'm back. Sorry for taking so long." She actually looked at Black-Star and cringed at the blood on his face. "Are you alright?" she exclaimed.

"Pah! This is nothing for a God," retorted Black-Star.

"And check you out! You took down Masamune!" He ignored Tsubaki's blush and held out his arms. "A God must reward good deeds, so here! A big, Black-Star hug for ya!"

Wordlessly, Tsubaki threw her arms around him and gripped him tightly. Grief and sadness she didn't even know she'd been holding back burst forth, and she cried into her meister's chest.

Black-Star just patted her head and said, "See! Your God made it better!"

At that, Tsubaki giggled through her tears.

Suddenly, the ground shuddered, and Tsubaki finally noticed the chaos that had set in around them. She looked behind Black-Star and saw the colossus attacking the city.

Tsubaki pursed her lips nervously. "Umm ... Black-Star, shouldn't we get in there and help?"

# 14 | Nyarlathotep

As Black-Star and Tsubaki engaged Masamune, the forest of shadowy spines blocking the path faltered. Maka and Kiddo slashed through them and sprinted down the now clear street. Maka took the lead toward the warehouse, from which Shaula's foul stench wafted. Every step she took closer to the building made her feel queasier. Three-dozen souls, mind-slaves to that Witch, resonated with ever-increasing focus. From within that hum, a pollutant started to spread, muddying the waters of Maka's resonance like an oil spill.

When they finally reached the warehouse, Maka stopped dead in her tracks. The resonating souls vanished. All she could sense now was that slick, overbearing stench of madness.

"We're too late!" she gasped.

Suddenly, the building's outer wall expanded and burst. Maka was thrown into the air. Kiddo caught her and brought his hover board to rest on a building nearby. They beheld the wrecked warehouse, filled with horror and rage. Clouds of smoke and dust shaded the night sky in tones of black and dark purple. A sinister light within the chaos began to take physical shape.

A hide of pale, mottled skin was stretched tight over an array of planet-shattering muscles. Four powerful legs crushed the surrounding buildings as the creature found its footing. Extending upward from those legs was a torso riddled with spiked tentacles and two burly arms having six fingers on each hand. Crowning the sight was a head that had only a jaw, which beared fangs dripping with red saliva. A pharaoh's headdress, made from plates of razor sharp metal, was melded into the beast's head, obscuring any hair, ears, or eyes – if it even had any.

From his perch in the aerie of DWMA, the Reaper chirped, "Been a while, ol' Nyarlie!"

The creature responded with a deafening roar.

Maka's legs felt weak, and she fell to her knees. She grasped onto Soul for support, unable to push through the dull noise that ripped through her resonance link. The creature's roar instilled in her an almost irresistible desire to bite, scream, cut, and flay.

"Snap out of it, Maka!" bellowed Kiddo. She looked up at him. His eyes were twitching ever so slightly. The creature's madness energy was getting to him as well. But the pursing of his lips and his stable breathing told her he was handling it.

"Maka, we need to get Shaula!" said Soul. His blade darted in the direction of the Witch, who stood before Nyarlathotep. Her braid glimmered sinisterly, and the monster's muscles twitched in response.

"It's her spell that unlocked the Trapezohedron," said Kiddo. He eyed the purple gem, shining radiantly amid a circle of burnt up corpses. "The device is still active. Meaning part of Nyarlathotep might still be stuck inside the pocket dimension. If we neutralise her, it might cause the gate to close and draw him back."

Maka eyed Soul. The eye on his scythe blade glared right back at her.

"C'mon, girl, let's go!" he yelled.

The image of Abhilasha's blood gushing from her self-inflicted wounds coursed through Maka's mind. She grit her teeth, pulled herself to her feet, and said, "Kiddo, Liz, Patty, keep Nyarlathotep distracted. I've got some students to avenge."

Kiddo took off on his hover board, and proceeded to blast Nyarlathotep with all his might. Maka leapt off the building, rolled on the asphalt to break her fall, and sprinted through the wreck toward Shaula. She twirled Soul around and let out a furious roar. Shaula flipped through the air, narrowly dodging Maka's blow. She countered with a fiery blast that knocked the meister back.

Shaula paused. Her cyan orbs glared at Maka, looking her up and down.

"Maka Albarn," chortled the Witch. "I do believe we have never been introduced." The Witch posed sassily for her opponent, her menacing braid flagellating behind her head. She drew her index finger up from her hip, past her breasts, along her neck, to her chin. Maka felt Soul shudder. A wave emanated from his spirit that made her skin crawl.

"The Hell, Soul?" she snapped. "You're acting like you're looking at Blaire again."

"I know, she's an evil hag," retorted Soul. He started to stammer. "But ya gotta admit, hag pretty hot!"

"Oh, thank you, Mister Scythe," chirped Shaula.

"Jesus, Soul! That bitch killed students," cried Maka.

"You're right," Soul gasped. Maka felt him stabilise. It took a little too long for her liking.

"Frigging pig," intoned Maka.

"C'mon, Maka, let's get her!" retorted Soul.

Maka lunged forward and swiped at Shaula. The Witch dodged and darted around her attacks, and then came at her with the poisoned braid. Maka swatted the wretched appendage aside, only to have it wrap around Soul's handle and yank her toward her enemy. Shaula head-butted Maka, making precise and painful contact with the young meister's nose. With a wave of her hands, Shaula formed dual pronged daggers. The blades whipped through the air between the combatants. Maka diverted Soul around her body to block the attacks, but Soul wouldn't stop shuddering. He made a slight misstep, giving Shaula an opening to jam her dagger in Maka's arm. The Witch targeted the wounded meister with her braid again, but Maka leapt back just in time.

"Damn it! Stupid Soul!" cried Maka. Sharp pain streamed through her arm, and blood dripped to the ground beside her.

"It's not my fault, Maka," yelled Soul.

"You keep getting distracted because you think she's hot," retorted Maka.

Shaula grinned lasciviously, "Oooh, are you not woman enough for your man, Miss Albarn?"

Maka's hair stood on end. She let out a manic roar and attacked. Her fury left her in endless shouts and clangs of Soul's blade against Shaula's daggers. And yet, despite the onslaught, Shaula still found time to make eye contact with Soul's reflection in the blade, and wink suggestively. Maka felt a wave of arousal trickle from his spirit, and it only made her angrier. She screeched and embedded Soul's blade in the asphalt.

Shaula landed a few metres away and chuckled as Maka wrenched Soul out of the ground.

"Jesus Christ, Maka! Calm down!" snapped Soul.

"Shut up, you frigging sleazebag!" bellowed Maka. "The city's being destroyed by Nyarlathotep, we're fighting the whore responsible for Abhilasha and Tamika, and all *you* can think about is her boobs!"

Shaula chimed, "Is that any way to treat an ally, Miss Albarn?" The Witch eyed Soul and said, "I never treat my friends that way."

"You have slaves, not friends," retorted Soul, though there wasn't any real emotion to his voice, and Maka could sense it.

"Oh, but Masamune is my friend," replied Shaula. "I'm so nice to him. I make him feel like he's swimming in silky chocolate. And I *never* belittle him for staring at some nice boobies. Or hit him for no reason at all."

Maka felt her resonance link with Soul waver. Her eyes darted between his blade and the enemy, and she grew very anxious.

"Hey, don't try to poach my weapon!" she snapped.

"Then do a better job of keeping him," retorted Shaula. She waved her arms, and three fireballs materialised in the air around her. With a flick of her wrists, she blasted them at Maka. The meister managed to dodge the first two, but the third hit the ground right beneath her feet, and sent her flying into the air. She soared over rooftops, and dug Soul's blade into one to stop her descent. She hung from his handle, her wounded arm sore and limp.

"Soul, how're we going to beat her?" she cried. "She's too strong."

Soul didn't reply. He just huffed, and returned to human form, leaving Maka to fall into a dumpster in the street. She scrambled out of the dumpster, shrieking and gagging at the stench around her. She saw Soul land gracefully on the street. He gazed over at Shaula, who stood in the middle of the road. He then turned to Maka and sneered at her.

"Screw you, Maka," he droned. "I'm goin' with Shaula."

"What?" exclaimed Maka.

"Comeuppance!" bellowed Shaula. She sauntered over toward Soul. "It's what you get when you just cry and demand and abuse, little girl."

"The Hell it is! You just cast a spell on him, didn't you?" growled Maka.

"Bitch, please," said Soul. "Do you see one of them white stabs on me? I ain't a mind slave. I'm just sick of this. I came to DWMA to be a Death Scythe – the consummate cool guy. I figured, go with the daughter of a Death Scythe, and I'll be on easy street. Sure, put up with her nerdy bitchiness. Small price to pay, eh?" His red eyes glared at Maka, full of disdain and frustration. "Then you screwed it up with Blaire. And we had to start all over again. And all you do is bitch and beat me up over *your* Goddamn daddy issues." Tears started to trickle down Maka's face, but Soul didn't let up. He took his place beside Shaula and barked, "Besides, who would choose a flabby flatty like you?"

Maka broke down.

"Go to Hell!" she cried. "After all that? After telling me, 'We'd get her!' You just jump on the next train? You get to be a Death Scythe, and then you just abandon the person who got you there? Leave her to be eaten alive by tumours while you get some whore to blow you! All of you men should just fucking die!"

Her eyes unleashed such a torrent, she could hardly open them. Every fibre of her being shook with betrayal, and she hung her head in dismay.

"Soul, you want to know why I'm such a bitch?" she moaned. "What else can I be when all you men do is hurt me? You asshole!"

Soul grinned and slung his arm around Shaula.

"Pah, what should you be?" he retorted. "How about cool like me?"

A sharp sound bisected the air about Maka's ears, and her eyes flew open. There was Soul's scythe arm, girdling Shaula. Her green eyes met his deep red orbs, and saw his determination. He held out his other hand and roared, "Maka!"

Maka's body took on a mind of its own and raced forward. She locked hands with Soul as he transformed. And she swung with all her might. Panic filled Shaula, and she dove for the ground. But she wasn't fast enough. Soul's blade skimmed the skin of her back, hooked under her braid, and sliced it off.

Shaula writhed and screamed on the ground. Her braid dropped to the asphalt and disintegrated in a puff of smoke.

Near DWMA, Nyarlathotep faltered. The creature's rampage, which had left a straight-line path of destruction directly to the Reaper's fortress, came to a grinding halt. Kiddo stopped mid-air and saw wispy tendrils emerge from Nyarlathotep's joints. They grew in number and brightness, before suddenly vanishing. The creature seemed confused, and it gazed around as if searching for its bearings.

"No!" cried Shaula. Now, it was her turn to cry at Maka. "You ruined my control of the creature!"

"And now *we're* gonna kill you!" retorted Soul and Maka. Shaula still had her speed. She darted out of Maka's path and leapt through the air toward Nyarlathotep. She stood before the beast and yelled, "Crawling Chaos! It is I, Shaula Gorgon, who freed you! You must obey me!" Her ruined hair and clothes did far less to her credibility than did her desperate expression. The beast just snarled and swiped at her.

The Witch flew, at a meteoric speed, out of the city and toward the horizon. Maka and Soul watched the woman soar, and could have sworn that she twinkled as she disappeared.

"We should probably go after her," intoned Soul.

"We've got bigger fish to fry," said Maka. She glanced over at the destroyed warehouse. The Trapezohedron lay in pieces, dark and inert. "The seal must be completely broken. We can't return him to the prison now, so we'll have to destroy him."

"Then let's go," said Soul.

Nyarlathotep resumed his rampage. But this time, he was far less focused on DWMA. He just smashed everything he could see. Maka used Soul to pole-vault onto a nearby building and began skipping rooftops toward the carnage. Black-Star joined her, Tsubaki's chain-scythes in hand.

"Masamune?" asked Soul.

"Neutralised," replied Tsubaki. "I have the Uncanny Sword form now."

"Now let's get this mutha-trucka outta here!" barked

Black-Star. "I can't stand somethin' bein' bigger than me!"

With a smile, Maka tapped her radio and said, "Kiddo. We're on our way. Draw him away from DWMA."

"Roger that," replied Kiddo.

The Reaper's son zoomed into Nyarlathotep's field of view and fired harassing shots across his face. The beast swiped at him, but he was too fast, and nimbly manoeuvred around the gigantic claws. With Liz, he fired along its arms while striking its mouth with Patty. He came about and pulled back away from the fortress. The beast turned to see Maka and Black-Star, weapons in hand, and roared.

"Maka! Kiddo!" yelled Black-Star. "We've got the shadow control now. We'll hold him down and you two take him out."

"Wait, Black-Star," said Tsubaki. "I don't think we're strong enough for this form just yet. And Nyarlathotep is too big."

"We'll weaken him," said Kiddo. He swooped onto one of the buildings beside the creature. He reached out with his soul to his weapons, who shuddered with excitement.

"Let's get him, Kiddo," said Liz.

"Gnarly hoe step is gonna get busted," exclaimed Patty.

Kiddo pointed the guns at the creature. The three yelled in unison: "Soul Resonance."

The air around them caught fire. Liz and Patty transformed into those gigantic cannons and spewed forth a devastating barrage. Nyarlathotep shrieked in alarm as the wavefront of Kiddo's attack threw him into the ground. Yet he didn't let up. He, Liz, and Patty let out a fierce roar and threw even more of their power into the blast.

"Black-Star, now!" yelled Kiddo.

Black-Star grinned excitedly. "Let's go, Tsubaki! Uncanny Sword mode!"

Tsubaki's chain-scythes glowed black and formed into

the dark blade. Together, they yelled: "Soul Resonance!" Masamune's black tattoos snaked across Black-Star's body and his eyes flashed blood red. With a roar, Black-Star thrust the blade into the ground, and the earth bled an inky black shadow. It scrambled across the ground with all speed toward Nyarlathotep, and enveloped him in a net of shadows.

"Maka, it's our turn," said Soul.

Maka looked to the blade, and saw his reflection smiling at her. She smirked, "You played me, didn't you?"

"Like a piano," said Soul. "To Hell with your Dad. Doesn't matter whether you're a man or woman. Form don't matter. What matters is the soul."

Maka smiled warmly. "Thank you, Soul."

Triumphantly, she twirled the scythe, and then wound herself up for a devastating blow.

*I can't remember the last time we did this,* she thought giddily.

They roared so loud the whole city could hear them: "Soul Resonance!"

The Earth pulsed, and Nyarlathotep gasped in horror of what was about to befall him. Maka stood before the creature, radiating the pure energy of her resonance with Soul. That bright blue fire formed vibrant wings about her body, as Soul's scythe blade grew larger. It started to glow, and grew a menacing face, its jaws hungry for flesh.

Their cries hit a zenith, and they were ready. Maka raced toward the struggling creature, leapt into the air, and brought Soul's massive glowing blade straight through the beast's head. The impact let out a shockwave that radiated through Nyarlathotep's body. From within his flesh, a blue light shone, which ripped the creature apart.

When the smoke and dust cleared, there was just silence. Maka slumped on the ground, completely drained. Soul assumed his human form and held her against his shoulder. Kiddo landed beside them, and Liz and Patty took their human forms. Tsubaki trudged toward them, shouldering a very exhausted Black-Star.

"The Uncanny Sword form seems to take a lot out of him," she said.

Maka looked around at the chaos. The road was hardly visible beneath the devastation. Homes, offices, businesses, and cars had been reduced to rubble. The sight just made her feel depressed.

Then, people trickled into the scene from adjacent streets. DCPD choppers floated overhead, while surviving meisters and weapons from Kiddo's security forces emerged from the rubble. There were lots of injuries, to be sure. But there were a lot of smiles too.

The crowd started to applaud, and it spread like wildfire, until all Maka could hear was their cheers.

## 15 | After Party

Kiddo stood beside his father, and gazed into the mirror. It showed a view of Death City. A month had gone by, and already the clean up was finished. Several homes and business had been lost, but the people were taking it in stride. Of course, it helped that the Reaper was subsidising all the victims until they got back on their feet.

"Such is the nature of humans, Kiddo," chuckled the Reaper. He tasselled his son's hair, much to the neurotic boy's irritation. "So, what did you think of those four?"

Kiddo harrumphed, "They were bothersome: quarrelling over nothing, nit-picking everything, and constantly trying to one-up each other. I'd doubted they could have come together."

"And yet they did," chirped the Reaper. "And they beat ol' Nyarlie too. Never thought I'd see that."

"Albarn is particularly strong," said Kiddo.

"'Course she is!" bellowed Spirit, who sat on the steps of the dais, eating a late lunch. "She's my Maka, after all."

"Actually," interjected Kiddo. "I'd say she's become strong for Winona." Spirit choked at the mention of his wife's name. Kiddo shrugged, "As for you, she just wants Soul to surpass you."

"It's true, Spirit," chuckled the Reaper. Spirit sneered at the two of them and went back to eating his meal silently.

The Reaper turned back to Kiddo and asked, "So, are you going to work with them again?"

"If I need to," said Kiddo, though he couldn't keep a smile from his face. A thought occurred to him, and his eyes darkened. "I may need them if someone else decides to unleash a monster upon us again. Father, I feel I should know if there is anything else in this castle that could be a liability."

The Reaper was silent. Then he gave a long, nasal hum. He blurted, "Not that I can think of, Kiddo."

Kiddo's yellow orbs fixated on his father a moment longer, but the Reaper didn't budge. He sighed, "Well then, if you think of anything, I would like to know immediately."

"Ordering your Daddy around now, are you?" chided the Reaper.

"Yes," said Kiddo. "Our organisation is supposed to be responsible for the darkest and most dangerous powers. And we've certainly done better than the Alchemic Regiment, and let's not even consider the Clow Cards. Nevertheless, we're the front line, and Nyarlathotep almost destroyed us. And we still don't know where Shaula is. I feel like I need to be ready for whatever happens."

The Reaper waved him off.

"It's alright, Kiddo, I was joking," he said. "But there's one thing I'm kinda glad for."

"What's that, Father?" intoned Kiddo.

"You've got some more friends," said the Reaper. "Liz and Patty are lovely gals, but it's always good to have more."

Kiddo chuckled, though he maintained his composure. He had to admit, it was nice to have people to think about. At the very least, his four new allies kept his mind off symmetry slightly more often than before.

"I just remembered, Maka and Soul were going to host a victory party," he said. He swivelled to leave the room, biding his father and Spirit a good evening. The Reaper's weapon stood, stretched, and took his leave as well.

The Reaper sighed contently. Then he turned, waved his comically large hands, and the mirror rippled. The image of an eighteen year old, with the slightest twinge of red to his hair, appeared before him.

"You were right, Eriol," said the Reaper. "Happened exactly as he predicted."

"Clow didn't predict everything, Lord Reaper," said Eriol, his thick Scottish accent simmering through the channel. "Plus, there's plenty of room in the plan for our own decisions and designs."

The Reaper hummed and scratched the side of his mask. "Listen, I'm not so comfortable with more than one being pulled in to this at once. How about Maka and Soul? They'll be fine."

"Considering the Lee Clan, it'll be a far cry to have Sakura's guardians involved," replied Eriol. "Plus, I have no idea whether Nathan Grant really is the one Clow predicted."

The Reaper waved his hand. "Whatever. Let's just make sure that everything is in order when the time comes."

Eriol pursed his lips nervously. His normally focused gaze faltered, and the Reaper felt exactly the same as he did. But they both knew there was nothing they could do about it. It was the plan they had both agreed to in another lifetime.

The ball was in motion, and all they could do was play their parts.

\* \* \*

Black-Star leaned back with a contented sigh. He rubbed his very full stomach and burped.

"That was a good feed!" he exclaimed. "Too bad about the taste though. But I'm stuffed!"

Maka sneered suspiciously at the ninja as he reclined on the couch in her and Soul's apartment. Tsubaki giggled beside her, while Liz and Patty anticipated some kind of rant and grinned excitedly at the prospect. Soul bussed the plates from the table and dropped them in the sink. He stopped by the fridge on the way back to the table, bringing two bottles of cider with him. He handed one to Kiddo, who had spent most of the meal gazing around the apartment.

"This is a very nice apartment," he intoned after his first sip of cider. "Everything's so orderly."

"Yeah, Maka nags me if I don't keep things tidy," said Soul.

"You have no idea how long it took to train him," jibed Maka as she poured cups of tea for the girls.

Liz's eyes brightened and she grabbed Maka's hands. "Please teach me your secret!"

"Why? Are you trying to kick Kiddo's symmetry addiction," asked Maka.

"No," said Liz. She glared at Patty. "I need to get this one to help around the house."

Patty punched the air. "Cleaning's boring! Makes me snore! Oink! Oink!"

"That's not what snoring sounds like, Patty," said Tsubaki with a frown.

"Yeah, don't bother," said Liz.

Suddenly, Maka's bedroom door flew open, and out sauntered Blaire. She wore her human form, but little else than a towel. She pouted suggestively and cooed, "Hey, does anyone want to have a shower with me?" She held her arms out welcomingly, only to allow the towel to fall to the ground.

Every jaw dropped. Kiddo and Black-Star cried, "Does this happen every day?"

Soul buried his red-hot face in his palms. "Will someone get rid of this freaking sex-crazed cat!?"

"Blaire! Clothes or cat form!" snapped Maka.

"But Maka," stammered Black-Star, whose face was turning blue. Blaire winked at the ninja, but that just made

Maka madder.

"Now!" yelled the blonde.

The voluptuous woman vanished in a puff and a black cat took her place. The cat harrumphed, her nose turned up at Maka, and trotted out on to the balcony and out of sight.

"Maka, seriously, why is she still here?" cried Soul.

"More importantly, why was she in *your* room?" asked Kiddo.

Liz's cheeks turned blood red, and she shot daggers at Kiddo. Meanwhile, Tsubaki and Patty had disappointed looks on their faces.

"Screw it!" exclaimed Soul. He walked over to the TV and switched it on. He tossed a blue Nintendo Switch controller to Black-Star and grabbed the red one. "Let's get that bastard that always beats us?"

"We're going after *him?*" asked Black-Star, an excited gleam in his eye.

"Who?" asked Kiddo.

"There's this mutha-trucka in Japan called *Hellhound99,* and he always beats us in Smash Brothers," yelled Black-Star.

"But I've been practicin', and I'm gonna get him this time," snarled Soul.

Maka sprinted to the TV and switched it off. She put her hands on her hips, very nanny-like, and chided, "You can't now. Otherwise, we'll be late."

"For what?" complained Black-Star.

Maka glared at Soul. "Did you forget? *The Creaking Coffin?*"

At that, Soul raced to his room and threw on his jacket. Tsubaki and Black-Star also whipped into action and donned their shoes. Kiddo, Liz, and Patty frowned with confusion.

"Come on! After party!" yawped Black-Star.

"You'll like this," added Maka with a smile.

The group left the apartment, Soul leading in a brisk

power-walk. They reached *The Creaking Coffin* just as the sun started set. Bouncers were having a hard time keeping the expectant crowd at bay, and it got even more difficult when they saw Soul and his friends trotting down the street. The manager let them in the back way.

"You're late," said the bartender with a smirk.

"Cool dudes're always fashionably late," retorted Soul.

The bar was full of patrons, all of whom cheered when Soul neared the stage. As he took a seat behind the microphone and tuned his guitar, Maka and the others pushed gently through the crowd toward their reserved spot.

Understandably, Kiddo was having the hardest time. There was asymmetry everywhere. He saw instantly the uneven numbers of men and woman, the dishevelled clothes on all of them, and the lop-sided nature of the bar's design. Liz and Patty's hands gripped his and kept him focused on Soul on stage.

Black-Star and Tsubaki bounced giddily. They'd looked forward to another of Soul's performances for so long.

Maka just kept her gaze on the stage.

Soul finished tuning his guitar and connecting the amps. He tapped the mic and stammered, "Testing. Ah, yep, that's good. Good evening, everyone. Soul Eater here." The crowd cheered. "Look, uh, it's been a tough couple of months for everyone. But I'm really glad you all turned up. I'm honoured to play for you tonight."

Soul directed his red gaze at his meister.

"My first performance is a crowd-favourite," he said. "I'd like to dedicate it to the coolest meister in Death City. She's the cute blonde over there."

Maka felt flushed as eyes darted her way, and people raised their glasses to her. With a smile, Soul began playing. His strumming hummed through the amps and down the street, followed by his voice, singing 'Karma Chameleon,' Maka's favourite song.

Soul played many songs that night. Every now and

again, he looked at Maka.

She never stopped smiling.

# Epilogue

The DWMA nurse had finished all of her work for the day. And yet, it was still the middle of the afternoon, and she was on call. Not that she minded. She scrolled down the webpage on her laptop, eyeing every single news headline that popped up.

A small rapping at the door pulled her away from the computer.

"Yes, come in," she said warmly. Two girls, no older than thirteen, stepped through the door. The taller one has long hair in a braid that framed her concerned face. She directed the shorter red headed girl by the shoulders into the nurse's office.

"Kim! Jackie!" chimed the nurse. "What's the matter?"

Kim wrung her hands nervously. Her brow was knitted, and she was clearly in a bit of pain. She couldn't bring herself to say anything.

Jackie decided to say it for her.

"It's that time of month, Nathalie," she said sternly. That made Kim cringe.

Nathalie's expression softened even more, if that was possible. She sat Kim down and went through checks of her vitals. She asked her questions with well-practiced tact. Then, she prescribed some pain relievers. Kim left in a much better mood than when she entered.

Nathalie's eyes remained fixed on the door a little

longer after the pair left. She smelled the hand that she'd used to measure Kim's temperature. The very subtle scent made her smirk with concern.

"First Shaula, then this," she mumbled.

She turned to her laptop and resumed her surfing. Then she saw a breaking news alert with the headline, *'Starlight Lancer confirmed – authentic footage!'* Her interest piqued, Nathalie tapped the link, and waited for the page to load. The video was shaky, but the events were unmistakable. An Australian boy placed his hand to his chest in front of a horde of reporters and cameras. A flash of golden light burst from his chest and materialised into a lance, which he held above his head. He proclaimed, "I am the Starlight Lancer!"

Nathalie grinned almost psychotically. Her excitement grew so much so quickly. Her soul protection spell almost broke under the strain.

"Thank you, Mister Grant," she mumbled in a low growl. "Because of you, my plans can proceed."

Beneath her clothes, the serpent tattoos along her arms twitched.

\* \* \*

Shaula's eyes fluttered open. Wooden rafters greeted her sluggish awakening. Her heart started to race at the recollection of her last memories. She'd been flying through the air, barely conscious and heavily concussed. The ground had raced up to meet her, and then she was on a bed.

She looked around. The room was small, and a set of video cameras glared at her from the corners. She felt her hair. It was short and messy. She recalled the scythe blade slicing through her beloved braid, and screamed furiously.

At that, the door of the room burst open. In sauntered a lanky creature in a single-breasted suit. His round yellow head hosted a long nose and a set of beady eyes.

"Moon!" exclaimed the creature.

Shaula opened her mouth to speak, but got a strong whiff of something from the man. She had not smelled it in a very long time.

"A homunculus," she intoned. "What do you want with me?"

"Oh, my suspicious sorceress," chimed the homunculus. "Allow acquaintance with my association. I am Moonface, former first functionary of the League of Extraordinary Elects."

Shaula grit her teeth. "I repeat, what do you want with me, flesh-eater?"

Moonface smiled and waved her off.

"I view your vengeful venture veered from victory," he said. He sat on the bed and drew near to her. "Perhaps, this patient person can present proposals purposeful to payback?"

Shaula licked her lips as she processed his words. She looked fixedly at the creature, whose eyes grew smaller as his grin grew wider. She'd never trusted homunculi. She felt they were the ultimate contradiction: created to excise the worst of humanity only to exemplify it. Yet, as she sat with powers diminished, she saw something in this strange character: a promise of another shot at revenge. She could, at the very least, hear him out.

"What did you have in mind?"

# Appendix A | Witchese Language

This language is spoken by the race of Witches. As they are a dark race, their language is very guttural, and unpleasant to the ears of humans and other beings. Even homunculi have trouble listening to it.

## Phonology

The consonant inventory of Witchese is very limited, including mostly plosive and fricative consonants.

|  | Bilabial | Alveolar | Palatal |
|---|---|---|---|
| **Stop** | p b | t d | k g |
| **Fricative** |  | s z | ǩ ǧ |

There is also a lateral alveolar [l], a post-alveolar rhotic [r], and a glottal fricative [h], which assimilates to a glottal stop after back vowels. The palatal fricatives, [ǩ] and [ǧ] are written as 'kh' and 'gh' in non-linguistic discourse.

There are five vowel sounds, corresponding to the basic vowels of English: [a], [i], [e], [o], and [u]. They however can be realised differently. [o] is often realised as English 'pot,' but after [l] may be pronounced as in 'corn.' Similarly, [e] is realised as in 'pet,' but is pronounced as 'ey' before fricatives. At the ends of words, [u] is pronounced as in Japanese (a short, unrounded back vowel

— pronounce the word 'sue' without rounding the lips); within words, it is a much more rounded sound, as in English 'pool.' **[i]** and **[a]** are the same as in English.

## Morphology

Witchese is a highly agglutinative language, conveying its grammatical meanings through affixes to root words. These affixes are mostly prefixes and suffixes, but infixes are known in rare occasions.

The following are noun markers.

The suffix **−i** forms the vocative case, used when invoking a name (though not necessarily referring to it as a subject of a sentence). It can sometimes be used as a topic marker. E.g. **krudi** *The Lightning.* This affix is applied before other markers.

The suffix **−su** is used in conjunction with the vocative marker to address a subordinate. E.g., **agdaisu** *You fool.*

The prefix **ub−** indicates the accusative, being the object of a sentence.

The prefix **so−** indicates a locative. E.g., **sobol** *To you.*

The verb markers are as follows:

The prefix **ak−** marks the jussive mood, indicating an order. E.g., **aktegri** *Consume it.*

The prefix **dzi−** marks the indicative mood, a statement of fact. E.g, **dziadazk** *It is uniting.*

The suffix **−rig** is a negation marker. E.g., **Ez ğaktrig** *Not that brat.*

The suffix **−b** forms the mediopassive voice, similar to 'self' as an argument. E.g., **Us aktegrib** *That thing ate itself.*

## Dictionary

The following is a non-comprehensive vocabulary of Witchese.

| | | |
|---|---|---|
| **adazk** | *Verb* | Unite / Merge |
| **agda** | *Noun* | Fool / weakling / easy target |
| **blik** | *Noun* | Earth / Soil / Spiritual Strength |

| | | |
|---|---|---|
| **bol** | *Pronoun* | You |
| **ez** | *Pronoun* | That one over there |
| **ğakt** | *Noun* | Boy / Imp / Waste |
| **gtu** | *Conjunction* | Similar in meaning to English 'if' |
| **hai** | *Verb* | Receive / absorb |
| **ǩatezo** | *Verb* | Destroy / Annihilate |
| **krud** | *Noun* | Lightning / Electricity |
| **loetu** | *Verb* | Incinerate / Burn / Vaporize / Destroy |
| **lokt** | *Pronoun* | Where |
| **oğalra** | *Verb* | Disintegrate / crumble |
| **praz** | *Noun* | Box / Chest / Container |
| **raz** | *Pronoun* | We / These ones here |
| **tegri** | *Verb* | Consume / Eat / Devour |
| **tseg** | *Verb* | Invert |
| **tuag** | *Noun* | Fire / Heat |
| **us** | *Pronoun* | That one here |
| **zlid** | *Verb* | Return / give back |

## Concluding Notes

As we learn more of Witchese, these grammars will expand. There is still much to discover. Although the DWMA does keep extensive records, they are under lock and key. Without much cooperation between the Lee Clan, the Alchemic Regiment, and the Reaper, there is little intelligence on this language that can be shared. Until that time, we will continue our studies with what little information we have.

# About the Author

Craig Stephen Cooper grew up in Wollongong, New South Wales, Australia. At a young age, he quickly developed a flare for the dramatic, an obsession with various video games, and an aptitude for expressiveness.

In response to his desire to develop video games, his parents allowed him to study software engineering under a tutor while still in primary school. At the same time, he took dance lessons after school. He later decided drama was a path better suited to his love of storytelling, and studied speech and drama during high school.

While completing a Bachelor of Computer Engineering, he underwent practical and theory examinations for an Associate Diploma of Performance Art. During his Doctor of Philosophy in Telecommunications, he taught speech and drama to primary school children. As a member of the Fellowship of Australian Writers, he has presented workshops on storytelling and poetry, drawing on his speech and drama studies.

Cooper conceived of *The AXOM Saga* while on a train from Fukuoka to Nagasaki in Japan. Under encouragement from his friends, he wrote the stories with a passion to equal his first novel, *Final Flight of the Ranegr.*

He also dabbles in video game and mobile app development.

# About the Illustrator

Tessa Eden grew up upon the shores of Australia's sunny beaches, frolicking in the sand and exploring the beautiful underwater world. Her father being a software engineer, and mother an illustrator, it was natural that she would grow to combine the two, becoming a digital artist. She now spends her days painting digitally, and creating 3D animations and CGI for animation studios in Sydney.